Acclaim For the Legendary MICKEY SPILLANE!

"One of the world's most popular mystery writers."
—*The Washington Post*

"Authentic narrative drive and almost hypnotic conviction…set Spillane apart from all his imitators."
—*The New York Times*

"There's a kind of power about Mickey Spillane that no other writer can imitate."
—*Miami Herald*

"Satisfying…its blithe lack of concern with present-day political correctness gives it a rough-hewn charm that's as refreshing as it is rare."
—*Entertainment Weekly*

"A superb writer. Spillane is one of this century's best-selling authors."
—*Cleveland Plain Dealer*

"Spillane's books…redefined the detective story."
—*Wallace Stroby*

"A wonderfully guilty pleasure."
—*Tim McLoughlin, The Brooklyn Rail*

"A fun, fast read…from one of the all-time greats."
—*Denver Rocky Mountain News*

"Spillane...presents nothing save visual facts; but he selects only those facts, only those eloquent details, which convey the visual reality of the scene and create a mood of desolate loneliness"

—*Ayn Rand*

"A writer who revolutionized a genre [with] heavy doses of testosterone, fast action, brutality and sensuality."

—*Publishers Weekly*

"Sexy and frantically paced."

—*Chicago American*

"Salty and satisfying...will hit like a slug of Old Crow from the bottom-drawer bottle."

—*The Buffalo News*

"Machine gun pace...good writing...fascinating tale."

—*Charlotte Observer*

"Simple, brutal, and sexy."

—*Kansas City Star*

"As bang-bang as you'd ever want."

—*The Associated Press*

"If you think he has lost his touch or drained the well, read this one...the new one is better than ever. If you are a Spillane fan you will enjoy this one more than anything done before. It is fast-moving, easy reading, and has the greatest shocker of an ending."

—*Albuquerque Tribune*

"The socko ending is Mickey Spillane's stock in trade, and never has he done it with greater effect...Sensational."
—*Buffalo News*

"A swift-paced, pulsating yarn...which very definitely shows that Mr. Spillane still has control of his fast ball, plus a few sneaky slow ones for the change-up."
—*Springfield Daily News*

"Need we say more than—the Mick is back."
—*Hammond Times*

I had lain in the wet grass outside Buck Head Benny's shack where he was holed up with three of his gang of damned killers all armed with AK's and sawed-off twelve gauge shotguns, looking for more cops to kill. My backup was still a mile away and all I had was my .45 with four shots left in the clip and their door swung open with a tiny creaking noise and they all came out too fast. They were ready but they didn't know where I was until Buck Head Benny spotted me and raised the AK in my direction, but before his finger could tighten on the trigger I took him down and he spun into a crazy twist, the AK going into its staccato chatter with the spasmodic yank on the trigger dying men make and the chopper took out all of his killer buddies behind him.

Back then I wasn't afraid of anything.

Now even breathing didn't come easily…

SOME OTHER HARD CASE CRIME BOOKS YOU WILL ENJOY:

THE GIRL WITH THE LONG GREEN HEART *by Lawrence Block*
THE GUTTER AND THE GRAVE *by Ed McBain*
NIGHT WALKER *by Donald Hamilton*
A TOUCH OF DEATH *by Charles Williams*
SAY IT WITH BULLETS *by Richard Powell*
WITNESS TO MYSELF *by Seymour Shubin*
BUST *by Ken Bruen and Jason Starr*
STRAIGHT CUT *by Madison Smartt Bell*
LEMONS NEVER LIE *by Richard Stark*
THE LAST QUARRY *by Max Allan Collins*
THE GUNS OF HEAVEN *by Pete Hamill*
THE LAST MATCH *by David Dodge*
GRAVE DESCEND *by John Lange*
THE PEDDLER *by Richard S. Prather*
LUCKY AT CARDS *by Lawrence Block*
ROBBIE'S WIFE *by Russell Hill*
THE VENGEFUL VIRGIN *by Gil Brewer*
THE WOUNDED AND THE SLAIN *by David Goodis*
BLACKMAILER *by George Axelrod*
SONGS OF INNOCENCE *by Richard Aleas*
FRIGHT *by Cornell Woolrich*
KILL NOW, PAY LATER *by Robert Terrall*
SLIDE *by Ken Bruen and Jason Starr*

Dead STREET

by **Mickey Spillane**

PREPARED FOR PUBLICATION BY
MAX ALLAN COLLINS

A HARD CASE  CRIME NOVEL

A HARD CASE CRIME BOOK
(HCC-037)
First Hard Case Crime edition: November 2007

Published by

Titan Books
A division of Titan Publishing Group Ltd
144 Southwark Street
London
SE1 0UP

in collaboration with Winterfall LLC

Print edition ISBN 978-0-85768-309-0
E-book ISBN 978-0-85768-644-2

Cover design by Cooley Design Lab
Design direction by Max Phillips
www.maxphillips.net

Typeset by Swordsmith Productions

Printed and bound by CPI Group (UK) Ltd, Croydon, CR0 4YY

Visit us on the web at www.HardCaseCrime.com

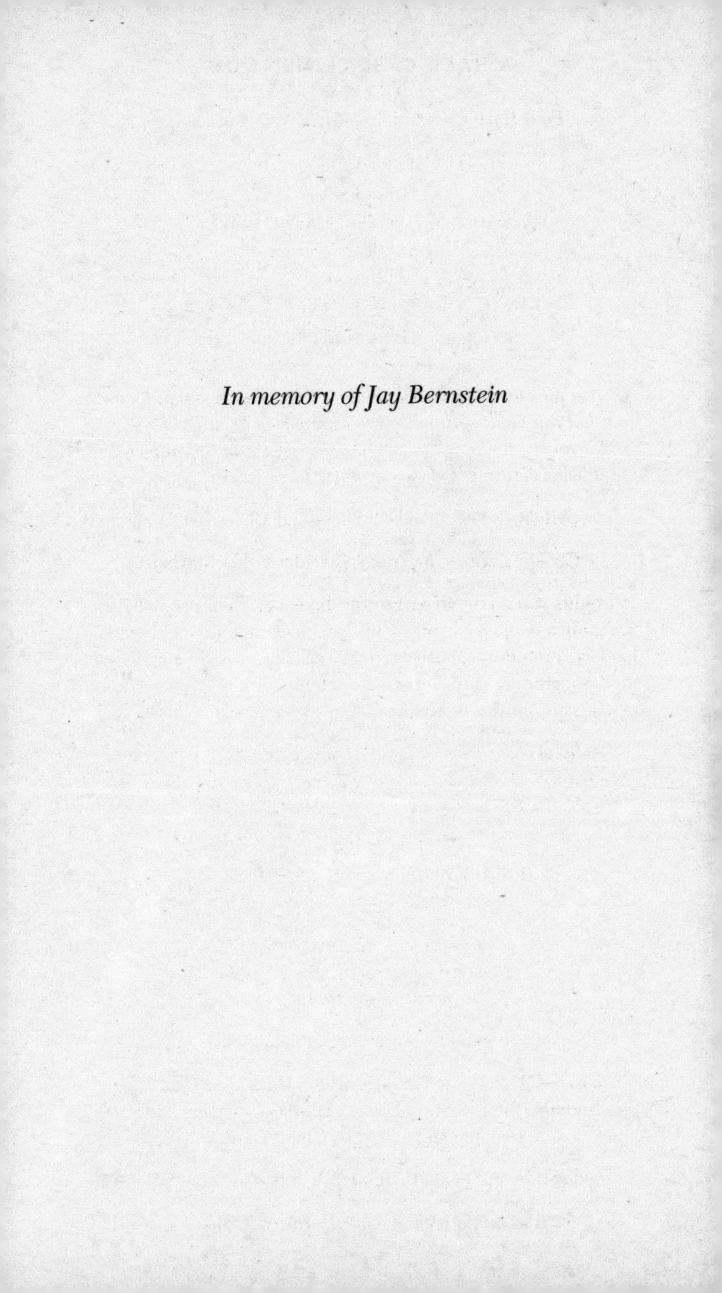

In memory of Jay Bernstein

DEAD STREET

Chapter One

The street wasn't dead yet. Not all the way. Old Charlie Wing had given the kids from the next block the last of the leechee nuts, and was packing his meager belongings for a U-Haul ride to Los Angeles and his relatives and then on by plane to his home province in China where he would be the richest man in the village and a big daddy to his horde of great and great-great grandkids.

Two houses down, the wicked witch of the neighborhood, ninety-year-old Bessie O'Brian, hung out the window, cushioning herself on a red velvet pillow as old as she was. When it snowed she stayed inside, only sliding the sash up if she heard gunshots. Hardly anything ever happened that she didn't know about. She saw Findley get killed, the cops nail the pickup truck loaded with five million bucks worth of narcotics, was able to identify over twenty muggers and was the State's foremost witness when Tootsie Carmody shot The Frog, the super peddler of heroin in the area. She wouldn't go to court to identify the shooter. She made the court come to her and for one day her tenement building was jammed past inspection requirements by New York's legal elite.

Bessie didn't wave. She just yelled down, "Kill anybody today, Captain Jack?"

"Not yet," I yelled back.

When I passed the brownstone where Bucky Mohler had lived, I could still see the faint outlines of the white *703* he had painted there when he was a trouble-making twelve-year-old punk. He had been knifed and shot twice before he was sixteen, then the Blue Uptowners nailed him with the radiator of a stolen car because he messed with one of their chicks.

That was a long time ago.

The Street was starting to die about then.

Set fifty feet back from the corner, so there would be ample curb space for a few squad cars, was the timeworn station house. It was an old-fashioned name for an old-fashioned building that had been born in the eighteen hundreds when this part of Manhattan still had goatherds and potato fields.

Until two years ago it had been well taken care of, but the financial cut-off had let the cement chip away from the courses of brick and left a blackboard for the damn graffiti artists to spray-paint insults on. A couple of those slobs were still wearing bandages. The station house wasn't going at full throttle, but the few left for roll call were the tough apples.

I used to be the boss man there. Captain. Hardass but fair. Good record. I got along with the troops and we kept the area as straight as it could get.

I retired out after wearing the badge for thirty years. I had gone into the Academy straight out of the Marine Corps back in '75, so I still had some good years ahead.

But I sure missed *the Job*.

It was quiet today. Overcast with a snap in the air. October was almost here and a fresh season of trouble was gearing up. Sergeant Davy Ross was standing beside an unmarked police vehicle, talking to a tall, thin guy in his fifties wearing black-frame glasses who had a white trench coat draped over his arm. In his hand was an inexpensive cardboard folder people keep receipts in and when Davy turned his head, glanced my way and said something, I knew they were talking about me.

Hell, I was the living anachronism, the old firehorse they couldn't get out of his stall, a dinosaur at fifty-six. Had to show up at home base the first of every month just to keep an eye on things.

Sergeant Ross grinned while we were shaking hands and said, "You got a fan from Staten Island, Jack. You remember that place?"

"Other side of the river, isn't it?"

"Roger. I think it still belongs to New York City, though." He paused and nodded toward the thin guy. "This is Dr. Thomas Brice."

When I took the doctor's hand, he said, "I'm a vet."

"What war?"

He grinned and the eyes behind the specs were alert and blue. "No, I mean I'm an animal doctor, Captain Stang. Don't want to get off on the wrong foot."

"No sweat," I told him. "I'm an animal lover myself."

Davy Ross cut in with, "You guys have your conversation. I'm going back to work."

We both told him so long and watched for a few seconds as he walked away.

When Dave went through the door, I said, "What's all this about, Doctor? You know, I'm not on the payroll anymore. I draw a pension."

Brice stared at me for a couple of seconds, his eyes reading me as though he were examining a strange breed of dog. It was an expression I had seen a lot of times before, but not from someone who didn't want to kill me.

Softly, Brice said, "Is there somewhere we can sit down? You must have a coffee shop around here somewhere."

I told him Billy's was down the avenue two blocks, an old cop's hangout that was about to go into the chopper when the station house shut its doors. Billy was finally going to have to go home and eat his wife's cooking for a change.

Two of the detectives from the other shift were winding up their tour and waved at me. Both of them eyed Thomas Brice with one of those cop glances that take in everything in a blink and they both had the shadow of a frown when they realized he was one of those clean civilian types and figured he probably was some distant relation of mine.

I winked and nodded back. They seemed relieved.

Over coffee and a bagel lathered with cream cheese, I said, "I haven't been to Staten Island since I was a kid." My eyes were cold and I scanned his face carefully.

"I understand," he told me.

"Neither do I remember ever having a case that involved that area."

His tongue ran over his lips lightly and his head bobbed again. "I know that too. I did some research on you and..."

"I'm clean," I interrupted.

"Yes, I know. You have a lot of commendations."

"A lot of scars, too."

I took a bite of the bagel and sipped at my coffee.

"It's a tough job, Captain," Brice said quietly.

"But nothing ever happened on Staten Island."

He was staring back at me now. I knew my eyes were growing colder.

"Captain, you're wrong," the doctor told me softly. "Something *did* happen on Staten Island."

I laid the bagel on the plate and under the table my fingers were interlaced, each hand telling the other not to reach for the gun on my belt. I didn't wear the shoulder holster with the old .45 Colt automatic snugged in it anymore. I was a civilian now. Still authorized by the state of New York to pack a firearm. But I wasn't on the Job any more. *Caution,* I kept telling myself. *Easy. Play this hand carefully.*

Something was going down.

And the doctor was reading me. His hands stayed on the tabletop.

For several seconds his eyes watched mine, but they were encompassing every feature of my face. Then Dr. Thomas Brice broke the ice. It didn't tinkle like a dropped champagne glass—it crashed like a piece from a glacier. "Long time ago, you were in love with a woman named Bettie…"

A pair of tiny muscles twitched alongside my spine. It wasn't a new sensation at all. Twice before I had felt those insidious little squirms and both times I had been shot at right afterward.

He was saying, "She was abducted and stuffed into a van but an alert had gone out minutes before and a police car was in pursuit. The chase led to the bridge over the Hudson River where the driver lost control, went through the guardrails and over the fencing and fell a hundred and thirty feet into the water."

My hand was on the .45 now. My thumb flipped off the leather snap fastener and eased the hammer back. If this was a pathetic jokester he was about to die at this last punch line.

Softly, I said, "There was an immediate search party on the site. They located the wreckage. The driver was dead. There was no other body recovered."

The doctor's expression never changed, the eyes behind the lenses unblinking. He let a moment pass and told me, "Correct, Captain, no other *body*."

Something seemed to jab into my heart. I waited, my forefinger curling around the trigger.

He added, "The next morning, right after dawn, one of the dogs in the cages at a veterinary clinic began whimpering strangely. It awakened the doctor—"

"A doctor named Brice?"

"Yes. But not this Brice—my late father. I was around, but not a vet yet. May I continue?"

I nodded.

"Anyway, my father got up to see what the trouble was. The animal was fine, but it was whimpering toward the rear lawn that bordered on the Hudson River. My father didn't quite know what was going on, but went with that dog's sensitivity and walked out the back."

Somehow, Dr. Brice read my expression. He knew that if there was a downside to his story, he was never going to finish it....

"There was a young girl there. Alive."

Alive!

"One arm was gripped fiercely around an inflated inner tube."

He must have seen my arm move. Somehow he knew there was no tense finger around the hammer of a deadly .45 automatic any longer.

"The night before, we had heard about the altercation in the city, and we both knew at once that this girl was the one who had been abducted. The late news mentioned that it was a mob snatch, as they called it, because sources within the NYPD indicated she had information that could seriously damage a major Mafia group."

"So you didn't report it," I stated.

"Fortunately not," he answered quickly. "My father checked with one of his friends on the local police force, who told him that the heat was on like never before and whatever that girl had could break up crime outfits from the city to Las Vegas."

"But nothing ever happened," I said. Something had rasped my voice. It sounded low and scratchy.

"Wouldn't have mattered," Brice told me.

"Why not?"

He let a few seconds pass before he said, "Because the girl...and she *was* a girl, twenty, twenty-one...had no memory at all of anything that had happened before the car crash."

And it was my turn to take a deep breath. "Nothing."

Dr. Brice shook his head.

I felt like vomiting. "Damn!"

"And that's not the only thing," he added.

"Oh?"

The eyes narrowed behind the lenses. "More than her memory was gone, Captain—she was blind. A terrible blow to her head had rendered her totally sightless. She would never be able to identify anybody ...or be able to remember her past."

"So she was no threat to the mob...."

"Come on, Captain. You know different. Until an identifiable body turned up, those people would never stop looking."

"That was more than twenty years ago," I reminded him.

Brice nodded slowly, his eyes on mine.

Before he could say anything, I let the words out slowly. *"Where is she?"*

He didn't tell me. He simply said, "That's why I'm here."

I knew there was a quiver in my voice when I asked, "Is she still alive?"

He nodded a *yes* and my pulse rate went up ten points.

She was alive! My Bettie was alive! I didn't care how she looked or how she remembered things, what she could see or couldn't see; my Bettie was alive and that's all that counted.

The old waitress came over, cleaned up what I had left of my bagel and refilled my coffee cup. I dropped in a couple of Sweet'N Lows and stirred them around. She squeezed my shoulder like she always did, and when she had walked away I asked the vet, "*Where*, Brice?"

"Safe," he told me.

"I didn't ask you that." There was an edge in my voice now.

"Can I finish the story?"

It was moving too damn slowly, but I wasn't leading the parade this time. It was his fifteen minutes of glory and, unless I wanted to risk slapping him around and losing his good will, I had to let him spell it out his way.

This is what he said:

"My father raised her. He nurtured her, cared for her in every way, educated her, made her self-sufficient in every manner imaginable. She was like a daughter to him."

"And a sister to you?"

Brice nodded. Then he leaned forward. "But there was always a little twitch in her memory, so to speak, that indicated she had a past somewhere. Not that it ever bothered anybody. In time even that went away."

"Did it?" I asked. "You're here now."

His smile was thinner than he was. "Very astute, Captain."

"Where *is* she?" I asked again.

"Safe," he said again.

"Where?"

"A prelude first…friend?"

"Make it quick. Friend."

"My father knew he was dying. The disease was incurable, but it gave him time to accomplish what he had to do."

"Oh?"

"His priority was to make sure Bettie was well taken care of. She had to be protected." He paused and added, "*Well* protected."

I nodded again, wondering where all this was leading.

Brice asked me, "Have you heard of Sunset Lodge in Florida?"

I bobbed my head quickly. "Sure."

He waited, wanting a further explanation.

"It's an SCS place."

When he scowled, I added, "Special Civil Service. A lot of the retired civil servants from the big city wind up their retirements there. Now they got the Jersey troops and the firemen in for neighbors."

"What else have you heard?" he asked me.

"Hell, they even have their own fire stations down there and the old cops are playing around with the kind of equipment we used to beg for. Man, the power of retirement voters."

"Florida loves them," Brice told me. "The cops all carry badges, legal but generously given, have permits to carry weapons; the firemen have all the best equipment and a real playground to spend their retirement years in."

"Who pays for all this?"

He didn't tell me. He simply said, "You'd be surprised."

We stared at each other across the table.

I finally said, "And she's *there*."

Dr. Brice looked at me sagely and nodded.

"She's safe?"

"Surrounded by experienced ex-officers, I'd say yes, quite safe. They think she is the wife of a former officer who died in the line of duty. And believe me, those ex-cops take care of their own."

"But she's blind...."

"Yes, and she lives alone. But her neighbors know her special needs, and those needs are surprisingly small. Anyone outside of this closed community of cops, well, she could fool into thinking she's sighted."

"Don't shit a shitter, Doc."

He shook his head. "I assure you, I'm not. Her physical actions...and reactions...are incredible. Her response to voices and sounds belies her blindness. She has a dog...not an ordinary seeing-eye dog, but a greyhound that had used up his running life on a racetrack. They were going to dispose of it until she took him in. That dog is her right hand and as friendly as it is, I'd hate to be a person who tried to attack her."

"Has anyone tried?"

"Not so far."

When the waitress came by again, I waved her off. Across the table Brice was watching me closely. But this was an old game with me and I played all my cards right.

I asked, "She lives alone, you say?"

"My late father bought a home outright, deeded it to her, established some investments that feed a healthy account in a local Florida bank that should take care of all her needs for...for as long as she lives."

The doctor didn't know that I could read eyes as well as I could. A tight grin was twitching at my mouth when I said, "But that's the issue, right, doc? As long as she lives? What's the rest of the story?"

A subtle smile turned the corner of his mouth up and he remarked, "I'm playing in your back yard now, aren't I?"

I just nodded. There are times when it's better not to say anything.

"My father left money in a trust and gave me instructions, in the event that I thought it necessary to...well, I bought you the house right next door, Captain Stang."

"What?"

He slid the folder he had been carrying over to me. "All the paperwork is in there. You also have a bank account opened in your name for one hundred thousand dollars. That and your pension should set you up pretty well. Just sign the papers and turn them in. I'm sure you'll know what to do."

I didn't bother to look. Crazy as it sounded, I knew what he was telling me was the truth and small shivers were beginning to run up my back. Not the money shivers. Not shivers from the owning of property. Just shivers from knowing that *she* was alive. *She* was twenty years older. *She* had a seeing-eye dog and now *she* was living next door to me. At Sunset Lodge. *Damn*.

Only I was twenty years older, too. And I'd always been older than Bettie, and…

No. Hell no. Age was gone. Age was something that was starting all over again. Starting now.

I grinned and wouldn't let Dr. Brice pay the tab. Not after his father's generosity—and his own. I laid a ten-dollar bill on the waitress' check, and we walked out.

On the sidewalk we shook hands solemnly and Brice said, "For a minute there I thought you were going to shoot me."

"For a minute there," I said, "I was."

Maybe he thought I was just fooling, but there was a cloud in his eyes. When I grinned at him the cloud bled away and he smiled back.

I know I slept that night. I didn't think it possible, but I did. I dreamed wild, exotic dreams that had vicious overtones because a face kept appearing that I recognized but couldn't identify and hot, mean hatred crept into that mental picture and I knew I would have to find that face because twenty-some years of life had been twisted into nothingness to satisfy his ambitions.

No, not ambitions—that wasn't the word at all. It was too damn scholarly.

Desires? No. It was more of a primitive, unhealthy

demand. Like rape. Disgusting, unnatural, vicious. Temporarily satisfying to the rapist but it was going to kill him eventually.

The face was there in my head and I couldn't make out the features at all. But I would. I would.

In the morning I went to the offices that housed the old files of known criminals, stuff that hadn't ever made it onto the computers, and sat at a table with three mugbooks dating back to twenty-some years ago and opened the dusty cover on the earliest.

Duffy Gross gave me a big smile and wanted to know if he could be of any help. I told him I just wanted to refresh my memory and saw him wink at Hump Bailey, another near-retirement cop, and knew what they were thinking. The retired ones never really come off the Job, they were thinking. Someone was always out there they had to catch. After the real heart-stoppers of wild chases and riotous shootouts, TV was dull, plain civilian life too damn quiet.

I said, "Don't laugh, wise guys—I might have a million-dollar joker in mind."

Hump muttered, "Sure, Jack."

Duffy did better than that. He added, "I still got three on *my* mind."

It was like going through an old photo album. There were a lot of faces you recognized, but today most of them would be dead or shriveling up behind bars. A few had gotten too old to be troublesome and were rotting away in a rocker somewhere on a back porch where the neighbors couldn't see them. Lucky neighbors.

I didn't find anybody I was looking for. I closed the last of the battered old books and put them back on the shelves and went downstairs to have lunch. But the face was still there. It was blank, but there was a word that could describe it.

Damn. Now I had to find a name for *it* and I didn't even know what *it* was.

Patience is something that cops learn. The initial eagerness of putting on a uniform is like training a puppy. All bounce and yips with lots of circles to run in. Ambitious, but without direction. Impatient, and after a lot of snags and pratfalls, he learns to look where he's going. He may get to use the acquired knowledge for a while, then all of a sudden he gets the retirement party and he becomes a sleepwalker people have to watch out for.

And Hump and Duffy were thinking that was just what *I* was, an old sleepwalker who couldn't get off the Job.

I went downstairs and walked over to Maxie's shooting range in the sub-basement of the Bryant Building, fired off a box of .45's, cleaned up and went back on the street again.

It was starting to rain.

A New York miracle happened on the corner when a cab stopped, disgorged a passenger and took me in before I had a chance to get wet. I gave him my address and leaned back against the cushions. There was a curious scent in the compartment, a mix of stale perfume, a touch of cigar smoke and the penetrating bite of gunpowder that still hung in my suit. It was a real city odor.

At my address I paid off the driver, said hello to the doorman and went up to my single-bedroom apartment. I turned the TV on to the weather channel, then kicked off my clothes, took a shower, half dressed again and eased into the leather La-Z-Boy lounger and watched the downpour wash away the dirty sins of the big city.

The apartment seemed practically new. When I lost Bettie, I got out of my old place that we'd shared briefly, where too many memories hung like a sweet smell in the rooms, and came here, a comfortable little warren with all the goodies of easy solitary living I could use and a few pieces of Bettie's furniture that had been handed down to her by her maternal grandmother. I slept in her four-poster bed and kept some of her clothes in my closet. Next to me was her favorite piece, a desk built back in the seventeen hundreds by a remote ancestor and just right for a small bar with eight bottles of assorted liquors. They were all full. Only the Canadian Club bottle had been opened. I stared at it for a few seconds, dipped a few ice cubes out of the miniature icemaker Bettie had given me, stirred in some CC and ginger and sat back to watch the pretty girl on the weather channel.

There were other faces when the commercials came on, and more faces when the news program started, but none were the face I was looking for. It was there, hidden someplace in the back of my mind.

It was a face that I could recognize from *then*, but this was *now* and I'd have to add twenty-some years to it.

I sipped at the drink, finally finished it, turned the light out and went into the bedroom. Tomorrow I'd have to start thinking like a cop again.

It had been one hell of a long day, longest since I walked away from the Job. But with Bettie back among the living, and back in my life, I was ready for more.

Chapter Two

It took another two days for the cop thing to really kick back in again. The walk that started out in the damp mist of an early morning wound through areas I was hardly aware of. Four times people remembered me and said hello with a small wave and I waved back and answered them, wondering who they were. None were very young. I had been away from this neighborhood for a long time.

The street sign didn't alert me. It was the store on the corner. It used to be a great deli where the salami was for real and the hard rolls fresh out of a bakery across town.

Now it was a small saloon with its own peculiar stink and a pair of cheap alcoholics waiting impatiently outside, squatting on small garbage containers. Unless they kicked the door in they were going to have to sweat out another four hours before the place opened. Legally, that is.

And suddenly there I was. Without conscious direction, my feet had taken me there, right down the sidewalk until I was standing outside the building that Bettie and I had lived in and I felt an unnatural coldness walk its way up my spine and I licked the dryness from my lips and breathed deeply for half a minute.

I had been walking in a fog. Time hadn't seemed to pass at all. It had been two hours since I left my place and I had hardly any memory of what streets I had crossed to get here. Nothing came back to me at all until I was outside the old apartment building where Bettie had been torn away and jammed into the back of a light truck.

It had been parked right beside the spot where I was standing. I hadn't been home that night, and I always wondered who knew I was on duty, because normally I was on days and had been filling in. The guys had come down the stairs carrying the rolled up rug with Bettie nearly smothering inside. They slid the old rug into the vehicle, slammed the doors shut and pulled away from the curb with the wheels screaming on the pavement.

The memory of it was almost as if I had seen it. Too many times the ugly scenario played out in my mind, but there was a hole there and emptiness is hard to define. The emotions of death and gruesome loneliness made it nearly impossible to penetrate that seeming vacuum.

But those emotions had suddenly evaporated and the big *why* suddenly appeared and hammered at my mind.

It was an *abduction* they had planned. Murder wasn't the objective. Bettie had something they *had to have*. It was something nobody else could give them. It had such importance that a mid-evening kidnapping had been executed regardless of the risk, but an insidious coincidence had raised its head and death came out of it.

Death for the abductors. They died.

Bettie was still alive!

*

Squirreled away in a folder in my apartment were all the details of the events of that night and Photostat copies of the official inquiries and the notes on lined pad sheets investigating detectives had made. The information was limited since Bettie had no connections at all with anything or anybody (with the exception of her cop boyfriend, yours truly) that would demand the terrible thing that happened to her.

The abductors' remains had been found, one body in the wreckage of the truck, the other a floater that turned up near West Point a couple of days later. Both had rap sheets filled up with petty offenses and a pair of entries that got them a few years of prison time, but the offenses were not related. Neither one had a driver's license or a credit card and according to persons who had known them, both were heavy drinkers, but there was no mention of drug use. One patrolman, who said he knew them both, reported that they'd do anything for a buck.

My notes were extremely sparse. I was officially listed as Bettie's fiancé and had no knowledge of her affairs at work at all. I had listed her occupation as the head of "Computer Input" for a company known as Credentials. Their main occupation was to verify the statements and background of persons seeking employment in reliable companies. A handwritten addendum stated that Credentials was in good standing with the local bank they used and the business outlets they dealt with.

I scowled at the information and shook my head.

Twenty years ago that word "computer" might have raised a red flag. But now? Hell, the kids in grade school were using them. I'd even had to learn to use the damn things myself before retirement kicked in.

There was a pamphlet at the bottom of the pages I held. Bettie's office group had held a party on the twentieth anniversary of Credentials being in business. I pulled out the phone book and looked the company up to see if they still were operating.

They were.

In the Yellow Pages too, and their address hadn't changed, either.

Bettie's picture was in the pamphlet. She was the prettiest one there. It was nothing formal, a semi-posed color snapshot and she was wearing a daringly cut outfit that was the sign of the times back then. Two of her lady friends flanked her, their smiles flashing into the camera lens. Kneeling nearby was the paunchy figure of her section boss and off to the side of the picture were three young kids, one in a short-sleeved shirt and a vest, another sporting flashy suspenders and the third apparently lying on the floor fixing something. From what little showed of his face in the photo, he didn't look happy at all.

There was nothing for me to see in the photo. It was over twenty-some years and whoever had been there then had probably moved on. I muttered "Maybe" to myself. Like Yogi Berra said, "The game ain't over until it's over."

At least Credentials was a starting point. I tucked

the pamphlet into my pocket, made a cup of coffee and got back on the street again. The rain had stopped. The clouds were still up there, but the pavement was drying off.

After a five-minute wait at the corner, a cab came by and gave me a ride to where Bettie had once worked. There were no sad feelings this time. Now I had Bettie alive and back in my life. In another day I'd see her. The airline ticket had been reserved and tonight I'd pack my bag.

At the office building I took the elevator up to the fourth floor and when the secretary asked who I wanted to see, I said, "Mr. Ray Burnwald. Is he still with the company?"

"Oh, yes," she told me. "And what is your name?"

"Jack Stang."

"You haven't been here before, have you?"

I grinned. "About twenty years ago."

She said, "Oh," like I was an old customer and buzzed the boss' office. When she hung up she pointed to a door and nodded for me to go on in.

Mr. Burnwald didn't look like the picture he had taken with the other employees. Age had touched him with a rough brush. Most of his hair had disappeared. His smooth face now drowned under the wrinkles of the years and the sport of hearty eating had given him a belt size in the fifties.

But there was still a sharpness in his eyes. They looked at me, they watched me for a split second and he was running my image through his mental computer. "I never forget a face," he said.

"Some I'd like to forget," I told him.

"You're not a customer."

"Right."

"You've been here before." It was a statement, not a query.

"Right," I said again.

"Cop," he said. It was a flat statement.

"Retired now," I said.

"It was when our poor Bettie was killed, wasn't it?"

"Sharp, Mr. Burnwald. You're a natural for this computer stuff."

"I know," he agreed. "What can I do for you?"

"Put that computer in your head to work. How much do you remember about Bettie before she was killed?"

Burnwald leaned forward on his desk, cradling his stomach on its edge. "I was only a section head then and had been Bettie's super for about six months."

"Any problems?" I asked.

"None. She was a very able person. We used to say she could even think like a computer."

"Computers think?"

"With the high-tech advancements, so one would certainly suspect."

"But not twenty years ago?"

"Well, they were on their way. Improvements were coming daily. New kids right out of college...and some even younger than that...were introducing developments that had unbelievable potential."

I nodded, thought a moment, then asked him, "Looking at it now, how does that 'potential' stand?"

He knew what I was thinking and his wrinkled face broke into a wry smile. "For its time, it seemed incredible. There are few words to express what it's like now. Only a genius can understand the workings of a computer today. And as for today's potential, it takes another computer to arrange any conversation at all."

"Bettie was smart," I remarked, "but below genius level."

"How would you know?"

"Because she was in love with me," I stated quietly. "Machines don't have love affairs."

"Not yet," he smiled. "Maybe someday."

"How would they enjoy it?"

"They'd think of something." He folded his hands together and leaned back in his chair. "And, unlike machines, geniuses can and do have love affairs...but I would agree—Bettie was bright, very bright, but hardly a genius. Neither am I, for that matter....What was it you really wanted, Mr. Stang?"

I didn't hesitate. "Describe Bettie's job to me."

This time he had to squint his face up and reach far back through the years and the improvements in computer product to recall the details of daily operations.

When he felt reasonably certain he had the scene in mind, he said, "In those days there were a lot of glitches. Nasty individuals would insert a virus into a system and wipe out computer operations for many hours. The anti-virus programs of today weren't even on the horizon. Also, there were a lot of normal breakdowns that could shut off power for major cities, causing near-catastrophic situations."

I bobbed my head and said, "I remember those days pretty well."

"Bettie was on a team of computer operators who investigated those events."

"This place had a *team*?"

Burnwald shook his head. "Not this place. Bettie was the only such expert here. The rest of the 'team' was scattered across the face of the United States. They were all in instant contact and had access to government processors that would give them any information they wanted."

Bettie had never mentioned any of this to me. I thought for a moment, then finally said, "Could that group break into government secrets?"

"I'm sure the federal people have their programs well-protected. But it wouldn't have been impossible for an expert like Bettie. Still..." He paused, put his folded hands under his chin and asked, "You're not accusing her of what they used to call...un-American activities."

I shook my head and let him see me smile gently. "I knew her pretty well, Mr. Burnwald. We were going to get married."

"Yes," he answered gravely, "and now she's dead."

I didn't bother to correct him.

"Is there anything specific you'd like, Mr. Stang?"

"A detailed rundown of her activities while she was here. Is that possible?"

"No trouble at all. I'll put one of our operators on it and she can retrieve it all within an hour. Can have it delivered to you this evening. Will that do?"

"You know," I told him, "guys like you could put cops out of work, couldn't you?"

"Certainly," he agreed.

"Only…who will shoot the bad guys then?"

"I'll check with our mainframe computer on that," he answered deadpan.

When I put my card in his hand, he studied it carefully before he remarked, "Ah, yes, now I remember you…Captain Stang. Or rather, your exploits. They called you the Shooter, didn't they, the media? 'A frightening figure to the mob,' or words to that effect?"

I shrugged and said, "That was a long time ago."

After a few seconds of silence during which Burnwald studied my face carefully, he said, "That time's back again, isn't it?"

My teeth were showing through the grin I gave him. I didn't have to give him an answer.

He knew what it was.

I didn't look for a cab this time. The sidewalks were great for thinking, like being in a lecture hall of a fine university. Knowledge and experience were all around you; there was traction and skidding, good and evil. All of it. In bunches. It was a great classroom of power waiting to be used.

Or misused.

I kept stepping off curbs and up onto curbs. Without realizing it again, I was walking a tortuous route to a place I knew well, letting my feet find it without giving them any conscious direction.

Finally, there it was, a street about to die. A pair of

big demolition units were parked fifty feet from the corner and four men in business suits, all carrying clipboards, were pointing out various areas and noting things down on their pads.

Outside Charlie Wing's building a small van was being loaded with his few possessions.

I stopped and said, "How's it going, pal?"

"Ah, Captain Jack," he smiled. His face was old and wrinkled, but he had the youngest smile you ever saw. "All goes good. Soon will be in China, Captain Jack. You ever be in China?"

I shook my head. "My war didn't take me any farther than Vietnam."

"You think things change for the better in China?"

"Ho ho ho," I said.

"What's that mean?"

"Keep your money in an American bank and your hands in your pockets."

He saw what I meant and nodded vigorously. "You smart man, Captain. I'll write you from China. You read Chinese?"

"I'll have it translated," I told him. "You be careful and stay out of trouble."

"Sure, Captain. Too damn old to get into trouble."

"Yeah?" We shook hands like the friends we were, then I let out a little chuckle and told Charlie Wing, "The heck you are."

"Heck you are, too, Captain Jack."

When the truck pulled away, I looked up and saw old Bessie O'Brian leaning forlornly on her window pillow waving at her departing neighbor, and when the truck turned at the corner and was out of sight, she wiped the tears from her eyes, then saw me and put her sentry face back on again.

"When are you going, Bessie?" I called out.

"I'm ordering my coffin today," she snapped.

"Come on, Bessie."

She let her eyes roam the street, then said, "My youngest daughter is coming to get me."

"From where?"

"Elizabeth, New Jersey. It's across the river in the country." She paused for a couple of seconds and added, "I hate the country. Damn, I don't even like Central Park."

"Why not?"

"There's animals there."

"Nah."

"The hell there ain't. People feed 'em peanuts and stuff like that there."

"Those are just squirrels, Bessie."

"I don't care what they are."

"Elizabeth is a pretty big city now. You'll enjoy it. Besides, you'll only be an hour away from New York. You can see all the big buildings with no trouble."

Her face drooped a little and she asked me, "Why do we all have to move, Captain Jack?"

"The street is dying, Bessie. We don't move out, we die with it."

"Be all right with me." She gave me a wry expression, said, "Watch out who you shoot, Jack. For a dyin' street, it's getting tougher around here all the time."

I nodded, blew her a kiss and walked toward the corner.

Bessie was wrong. There was no more toughness on the street now. The tough stuff had gone someplace when the street got sick. It left completely when the street threatened to heave a post-mortem sigh.

At the incoming of the one-way street they had already put up a NO THOROUGHFARE barricade. The other end was open. You could go out but you couldn't come in. Somebody had issued a quick exit move for the old station house troops and two city trucks were loaded with antique desks, swivel chairs, straight backs and coat racks. Another had nothing but file cabinets stacked from the cab to the tailgate of a rack-sided tractor-trailer.

The police personnel were all on duty, so they were holding down the telephones inside and collecting their personal items until they went off to other assignments. Bessie O'Brian would probably wave all of them off before they came and got her. Then the street would be dead.

But not yet.

I had to be the last to leave and that wasn't yet. The street would be dead, but somebody would have to bury it, and that was me.

Then the street would *really* be dead.

In my pocket the cell phone gave off a buzz and I switched it to TALK. Thomas Brice said hello and told me he'd pick me up in one hour for a trip to Staten Island. It was a trip I dreaded in one way, but had to make. I had to have every detail of that whole situation resolved in my head so there would be no errors. Twenty years of lost time could make for strange changes and I wanted nothing to hit me unexpectedly.

And Thomas Brice was right on time. We drove over the bridge and when I looked down I almost felt the sensation of falling that wild distance to the murky waters of the Hudson River. Traffic was thin at that hour and before long we were in that other, strange part of New York City that was like a different state to most Manhattanites.

The veterinary building was right on the edge of the Hudson itself, an old building from the eighteen hundreds, resurrected with concrete and brick and decorative wooden pillars, discreetly identified by a small sign over the main door and a pair of old oaken statues of a cat on one side and a husky on the other. Inside, behind the large glass windows, I could see a pair of white-robed attendants busy behind the main counter.

Brice said, "We're here."

I wanted to tell him tomorrow would be the *here* day, the day when the plane landed in Florida. Nothing else counted. This was only a preliminary show to get me up to speed.

A couple of times Brice glanced at me to see how I was taking it. I wasn't sweating. There was no catch in my voice. I followed him into the building, met the two attendants, then went through a pair of swinging doors into a neat animal hospital. But that wasn't what Thomas Brice wanted to show me.

The bedroom was in the very rear of the building

and the second I entered it I knew it had been hers.

There was a smell to it that belonged to her and the accoutrements on the wall shelves and the dresser top were exactly the same as she'd had in her own room years ago. That kind of taste apparently didn't have to be reacquired. I opened the closet door and again knew exactly who the garments hanging there had belonged to. Even the light fragrance hadn't changed.

Brice closed the door and turned to me. "You're sure now, aren't you?"

"Nearly," I told him.

On the bed was an old-fashioned photo album. Brice thumbed open the leather snap fastener and there in 5x7 color snapshots was my dark-haired, hazel-eyed Bettie. She was beautiful and unmarked and smiling a huge smile right at me. At nobody else, just at me. All I could say was a softly heard "Damn!"

She was still young, beautiful beyond belief, plainly dressed, but a total knockout. And yet a strange blankness possessed her features.

Brice was saying, "This was taken a month and a half after she was washed ashore."

"But..."

Brice interrupted: "She was like a newly born baby here. She couldn't speak, couldn't understand, but she showed emotions. She took to my father right away, like a newborn kitten responding to its parent's teaching."

My voice was barely audible. "Animalistic?"

"No," Brice reassured me. "Very human, but a fully grown, well-developed newborn child."

"There were no memories?"

"None at all."

I turned the pages of the album and watched Bettie develop, little by little, characteristics emerging step by step. I noticed the date on the photographs and saw that they were taken at regular intervals and understood that this was a medical case study by a competent researcher.

When I glanced up at Thomas Brice, he explained, "Going by what the police had released to the press, we knew that her life was in absolute jeopardy if this information ever got out. However, there were no relatives to contact, no inquiries made about her health and if my father hadn't seen a small blurb in the old *Sunday News* about you being on the case, we would never have known whom to contact."

"But you didn't contact me!"

"No. And I can understand your resentment. But the young woman you knew didn't exist. My father knew that exposing the woman she had been in any way would be enough to get her killed. We gave her a fresh start."

"Damnit, I could have—"

"Captain, I didn't make these decisions, my father did. And if you want to take it up with him, I'll direct you to the appropriate cemetery."

I said nothing.

"Contacting you someday was always a possibility. Dad did a lot of probing before he realized the truth and knew you two had planned marrying. He watched your career and came to know you were one of the honest ones."

"There are plenty of honest ones—"

"No offense, Captain. After all these years, I didn't know how you'd feel about your…your lost love. But I found that you were still single, even after retirement, and decided to follow my late father's wishes, and contact you."

After looking at the photos, it was hard to speak.

Brice asked, "Are you comfortable with all this?"

"Not completely," I told him.

"It's a lot to take in, I know."

"That's not it."

"What is, then?"

"Somebody has got to pay for twenty lost years."

"They may be dead."

"I'll kick over their tombstone," I said.

There were papers to be signed and attested to by witnesses and a Notary Public, papers issued by the bank to be affixed with my name, and when it was all over I was the legal guardian of a woman I had promised to marry two decades ago. My heart was beating a reserved tattoo. I left all the legal papers in Dr. Brice's office safe. Later I'd get a certified copy at my new address.

Damn, a new address? I hadn't lived out of state since I was a kid, and couldn't even wonder what it would be like. Then I'd have a picture of Bettie blossom in my mind and it didn't matter at all anymore.

And the transformation would be simple. There would be no debts to pay off, very little to pack and move, no big friends to say so long to and a happy retirement from then on.

Who was I kidding?

Someplace there would be a hole in the program. Something would crack, then it would split, and a sharp-nosed reporter would spot a story. *Ex-Killer Cop Moves to Sun City!* Or maybe, *Top Gun of NYPD Takes on Retirement Home!* There were tabloid newspapers that would eat that kind of thing up.

And then somebody would remember, and somebody would worry, and somebody would call in the shooter soldiers who carried modern artillery on their persons and have access to more sophisticated weaponry at their beck and call.

It didn't matter how many would be killed in the shootout as long as the main target was acquired and silenced permanently. And the main target would be plural. Bettie, then me. Or me first if they wanted to quell the firepower.

It took me two days to get everything in order. A single man doesn't get entangled in many things, so shipment was a snap. The moving company did it all. Two cartons, the disassembled four-poster bed, Bettie's old desk, my swivel chair and a few odds and ends, and I was ready to go. At the last minute I cashed in my plane tickets, deciding to drive and have transportation at hand all the time. A one-day trip to Myrtle Beach, South Carolina, then another day's drive to Sunset Lodge.

The end would be the start of the beginning.

Chapter Three

The two-day drive was an easy one. Traffic was sparse between seasons and at the beginning of the second day I got up before five, had a light breakfast and was on the road long before six. Seven hours later I crossed the Florida state line and stayed on Interstate 95 until I hit the east-west highway that would take me to Sunset Lodge. Along the way, the road passed the site of another complex named Garrison Estates that was still partly under construction.

A series of neat billboards set well back off the macadam highway told its story. There were no renters. Each dwelling was occupant-owned, oceanside swimming and fishing areas very accessible, police and fire protection adequate and privacy guaranteed, starting with a monitored gate entry.

Money had gone into this development, the kind that older people who enjoyed peace and quiet and an early-to-bed and late-to-rise lifestyle would enjoy. Several luxury-model vehicles passed me by, well-attired elderly in the front seat. In two of them a woman was driving. If Sunset Lodge was anything like Garrison Estates, I could risk a sigh of satisfaction with the good doctor's choice of residence for his adopted daughter, my Bettie.

The very thought of seeing her again made my heart

pound and I reminded myself that this had to be a carefully studied move. In my fantasy, she would see me and recognize me and all of those memories would flood through her and....

Right.

On the left of the road there was another area, neatly fenced off and identified by a sign that said GARRISON PROPERTIES—ONE OF FLORIDA'S EARLIEST PERSONAL ESTATES, indicating the part of the gated community that was still under development. So far, somebody sure had a big front lawn of sand.

There was nothing else to be seen until I had driven for another mile and saw the outlines of buildings a couple of miles off the road. There was another brick-gated entry with no attendant visible, but tire tracks were very evident in the sand, all leading on toward the low-lying buildings. Just a little way farther on, a half-dozen head of cattle were browsing amongst some visible greenery. They weren't any kind of cow I could name, but they sure could exist on desert delights. All of them were big and muscular-looking.

It was another twenty minutes of driving before the wire fencing appeared. It was the kind to keep animals out, not people. Another two miles and the first small billboard appeared on my right that read SUNSET LODGE—A TOTAL RETIREMENT RETREAT.

And I breathed a small sigh of relief. This place, even at the gated entry, spelled quiet luxury. From a distance I could see the pleasant shapes of small buildings and the sand sprouted acres of bright green grass. I stuck my head out the window, away from the air-conditioned atmosphere I'd been breathing, and took a deep sniff of the tangy, salt-laden ocean air. Outside the red-brick guard post was a neatly painted sign that read, *Yacht Docking and Boat Rental Facilities. Guided Ocean Fishing Trips. Crewed Scenic Sailing Tours Daily*.

The good doctor had really gone all out for his protégé.

The tan-uniformed attendant, carrying a clipboard in his hand, came out to meet me. He walked with the air of someone in total authority, disguised by neighborly friendliness. He said, "Good morning, sir—can I help you?"

He was a trim sixty or so with his blond hair cut in a military crew. I handed him the document of home ownership and his smile grew into something natural. When he handed it back he said very seriously, "Great to have you here with us, sir."

I took the papers, nodded back and said, "You're from New Jersey, aren't you?"

"Newark. Been retired three years. Name's George Wilson. My accent show?"

"To a New Yorker, absolutely." I stuck my hand out and shook his. "Jack Stang, NYPD, retired."

He scowled a few seconds, then gave me a big grin. "Damn, you're the Shooter, aren't you?"

I gave him a weary laugh. "That's what the tabloids called me."

"Didn't you off Creamy Abbott during that bank heist back in '82?"

"No choice," I told him. "He swung that AK at me and I had to pop him."

"Yeah," he laughed, "one shot right between the horns from fifty feet away."

"Pure luck," I retorted.

"Pure twice weekly visits to a gun range, pal," he said.

I made a face at that observation.

"Somebody around here was saying they just demolished an old station house back in the big city—was that yours?"

I nodded. "When I went, the old building went. Hell," I added, "the street went too."

"This place isn't Manhattan, you know. Think you'll like it here?"

I gave him a little shrug and answered, "Anything beats out city noise and multiple gunshots."

"Won't get much of that here," he told me, "except on the firing range.... Want me to have a car lead the way in to your place?"

I shook my head. "I'll find it. I used to be a detective, you know. I'll have to get adjusted to the area anyway."

"No problem. Streets are all in numerical or alphabetical order."

"I'll find it."

"Sure. You want me to tell the boys at the clubhouse you got here? You'll be a real surprise to them."

"The clubhouse?"

He pointed vaguely. “Can’t miss it. A big brick building with blue doors right in the middle of the shopping area. You want the right and left turns?”

I waved him off on that one. “Naw, let me handle it alone. I have to get settled in first.”

“Sure, Captain. I know how it is.”

“You can skip the ‘captain.’ I’m off the Job now.”

“We’re never off the Job, Captain,” Wilson said seriously.

Everything radiated out from the big early Floridian-styled building with the wooden chiseled sign across its entry that read SUNSET LODGE. I found the block I wanted and followed it halfway to its end. The stucco houses along Kenneth Avenue were one-and-a-half stories, bigger than the other homes I’d passed.

I saw number 820, Bettie Brice’s address, and my foot came off the gas pedal as though somebody had kicked it away. A few kids played beside other houses nearby, but 820 was quiet, empty. The front windows were half-opened and a UPS package nestled between the arms of a rocking chair on the porch. No car was parked in the driveway.

My heart started to hammer again as I eased into the driveway beside 818, then got out slowly and walked up the porch steps to the door. I put the key in the lock, turned it and heard it click open.

The place had a new, recently cleaned smell to it. To me a chair was a seat and a bed was where you slept, but someone had gone to a lot of lengths to furnish this place with truly masculine pieces. Nothing gaudy, nothing oddball, just masculine—with the exception of Bettie's old four-poster bed and antique desk, which had beat me down here thanks to the movers. Both were in the master bedroom upstairs.

I wandered through the rooms checking every item out. This was a house a man would have lived in, but furnished by a woman who thought a lot of him and his personal likes and dislikes. One of the ex-cops' wives down here had lent a hand on the decorating front.

In a sealed envelope attached to a few other papers was the description of a "secret" area in the master bedroom where I could store any weapons, ammunition or important documents I had. It had been built into the house itself, an area almost impossible to find unless you had a dog that could sniff out gunpowder or gun oil odors. Somebody had been thinking ahead.

I located the disguised wall section—paneling that was really a door—that revealed a hold for rifles and handguns, shelves for ammunition, ear mufflers for shooting on gun ranges, goggles, latex gloves, and pistol and rifle cleaning equipment. There were two heavy clothes hooks on one wall with a pamphlet selling bulletproof vests hanging from the nearest.

Even before I laid out my clothes, I pulled all my weaponry out of its case and deposited everything except my .45 and the old shoulder holster in its newly assigned hiding place. My well-oiled piece I kept right where I could reach it in a hurry on the nightstand. The gun and the four-poster bed made an unlikely couple. Of course, once upon a time so had Bettie and me.

Getting my clothes in the dresser drawers and the

closet took ten minutes, then I went to the kitchen. Non-perishables were stored in the pantry and the refrigerator held all the staples I'd need for a few days. The cooking utensils were stacked away, some still showing their price tags. Even the bathroom was in working order, with new soap cakes, rolls of toilet paper and plenty of new, white towels.

I tried the toilet bowl and it flushed perfectly. The faucets poured out clean, clear water and the drinking cups had paper hoods draped over them. Thomas Brice had made sure of everything.

I hoped he had made sure of tomorrow. I'd be seeing her then. When I thought of it I had to take a deep breath and hold it for half a minute. By then my heart rate had returned to normal.

The drive down had been more tiring than I had expected. My eyes were heavy and as early as it was I hopped into the shower, cleaned up, brushed my teeth and got into bed.

Some dreams are impossible to remember. They get scrambled and exist beyond comprehension. This dream was different. Bettie was outside my door. I could smell her perfume. She was staring at my door and never noticed the black draped figure tiptoeing up the porch stairs behind her. He was carrying a long-bladed knife in one hand and the other was stretched out to muffle any sound she tried to let out.

And I couldn't turn the knob! I couldn't get the damned door open!

I pulled and twisted but the knob wouldn't turn and just before I could let out an agonizing howl of despair my eyes flew open and I muffled the yell that nearly came out of me.

Sweat had drenched me. My pulse rate was incredible. It was five minutes before I went back to normal. This time I forced myself to sleep.

It was still dark when I awoke. In the east the sky was barely showing the first edges of light and I knew that in an hour a new time of life would begin for me.

I made coffee, had two cups, then got dressed, climbing into a short-sleeved sweatshirt and my old khakis and sandals and went out on the porch to watch the sun come up. In New York it would be late morning before it rose above the apartment rooftops.

From next door I heard the first bark of a large dog, a short, throaty good morning kind of sound the big ones make to get their owner out of the sack. Then there was just the muted murmur of a lovely girl saying something sweetly unintelligible to her canine pet and the wild beating in my chest was almost painful because I knew it was her! All I needed was any sound. One small sound and now I *knew.* Bettie was alive!

And now I was alive too.

But all I could do was ease myself to the edge of the old wooden rocking chair and sit there, immobilized by what was about to happen. I had lain in the wet grass outside Buck Head Benny's shack where he was holed up with three of his gang of damned killers all armed with AK's and sawed-off twelve gauge shotguns, looking for more cops to kill. My backup was still a mile away and all I had was my .45 with four shots left in the clip and their door swung open with a tiny creaking noise and they all came out too fast. They were ready but they didn't know where I was until Buck Head Benny spotted me and raised the AK in my direction, but before his finger could tighten on the trigger I took him down and he spun into a crazy twist, the AK going into its staccato chatter with the spasmodic yank on the trigger dying men make and the chopper took out all of his killer buddies behind him.

Then I wasn't afraid of anything.

Now even breathing didn't come easily.

Her door swung open and the dog came out, a huge beast for a racing greyhound. And he heard me. He didn't just sense me. His ears twitched as he picked up the sound of my breath, but there was no angry retort in his posture. For a second he was immobilized and I saw her hand come out, reach down and felt the stiffness in his stance and she said, "Tacos, is someone here?"

Only ten feet separated us. A million miles of ten feet and I had to squeeze in all those twenty years of thinking and dreaming about what I had thought was completely lost, then suddenly face it up close, only ten feet away.

She hadn't changed at all.

Her beauty was still untouched—shoulder-length brunette hair, the narrow oval face, the pert nose, the ripe full mouth. In a pink short-sleeved top and white shorts and open-toe sandals, she was fresh and vital and tanned, a long-legged beauty still seeming to emanate an invisible radiance and I knew it was something that only I would see.

I said in an unhurried voice, "I'm your new neighbor, miss..."

And something odd happened to her face.

It was a bee-sting reaction without any pain, a brief moment of total consternation, and if I weren't very much aware of what was happening, I wouldn't have noticed before she quickly returned to a perfectly normal stance.

A voice she hadn't heard for twenty years had been suddenly awakened in her memory, but it didn't last long. How many times before could that have happened? When another few seconds passed I knew that she had frozen the episode in her memory banks.

"I'm Jack Stang, ma'am. It's nice to see you."

My voice located my face for her and she looked directly at me without seeing a damn thing. There was no opaqueness to the pupils of her big hazel eyes. They were the same color she'd always had and when she blinked she kept every expression absolutely normal.

Few would ever suspect that she was totally blind.

She called back, "And I'm Bettie Brice from Staten Island! Mr. Kinder, the manager here, said you'd be arriving. I hope you enjoy Sunset Lodge, Mr. Stang. Do you have friends here?"

I let out a chuckle and nodded, even though she couldn't see it. "Oh, yeah, I have quite a few here already."

"That's nice," she said. Then she frowned and added, "For some reason your voice is familiar, but I'm sure we haven't met before."

"Well, we've met now," I told her, "and that's what's important."

"Yes, it certainly is," she answered, then gave me an airy wave and went down the steps to the sidewalk, Tacos, the greyhound, leading the way. He almost hugged her legs, alert to her every move.

When she stopped for a second it was as if she were going to retrace her steps, then she made a tiny shrug and went toward the end of the street.

Chapter Four

The new black Ford was identified with a lettered logo on its front doors that read

SUNSET LODGE
SECURITY

Beneath it in smaller letters it said,

Darris Kinder
Captain/Manager

All very simple. Nothing ostentatious. The only difference was the sound the engine made. It wasn't an ordinary Ford vehicle at all. This was a highly refined chase car that could match any vehicle the state of Florida had on the highways. The sound wasn't noisy. It radiated power. Maximum power.

Darris Kinder came out from under the wheel, scanned the area quickly and quietly and shut the door very softly. No dome light had gone on over his head when the door opened and I felt a touch of identity with the "Captain/Manager." He was a rangy, fifty-ish guy with a dark crewcut, light blue eyes and Apache features. When he walked up the path to my porch, it was with a military tread.

I held out my hand and said, "Semper Fi, Captain Kinder."

He grinned back at me and answered, "It shows?"

"Only to another old gyrene. Come on in."

Before he walked through my door he gave another long glance around the neighborhood, then walked in and parked himself in the big rocker.

I said, "How long were you a cop?"

"Fifteen years in Newark. Made Lieutenant before I got this deal offered to me down here. Instant Captain, a fivefold increase in pay and a budget bigger than a lot of cities set aside for their police departments." He paused, his eyes searching my face, "You had a great record, Captain Stang."

"Call me Jack. I'm retired, Captain."

"I think you know better than that," he said. "We never really retire, do we?"

My answer was silence and a grin.

"I always make courtesy calls to new arrivals, but you are not new to me at all. When Dr. Brice purchased Miss Brice's house, he made me a confidant in the situation that had occurred, and to what would happen...if any word of this leaked out."

"And?"

"It's not very comfortable," he told me.

"She's been here years," I stated, "and there've been no leaks."

"That damn pack of hoods never gives up. You know that. They aren't dumb, either. They were able to tuck old Jimmy Hoffa away in a place where all the resources of the U.S. Government couldn't find him. They influence political activity and control industrial actions through union membership and they don't take too kindly to anyone throwing a wrench into their machinery."

I thought for a moment, then nodded. "How thoroughly did you research the facts?"

"I didn't raise any red flags. The organized crime bunch haven't shown any interest. Yet. According to all recorded information, Miss Bettie Marlow died in the wreck of that truck in the Hudson River."

"Than you're the only one who knows she's still alive."

"You do," Kinder said softly.

"So?"

"I understand that she has something heavy that could wreck mob operations."

"That's what the ones who grabbed her suspected, not *knew*."

Kinder wiped his hand across his mouth and stared hard at me. He said, "I found out a certain Mafia family kept a close watch on all your activities for twelve years after her supposed death to see if you had acquired any information she might have had."

"I didn't acquire shit," I said, "and the mob boys know it. They're pretty efficient. We have our own sources inside their operations."

"They haven't given up, you know."

I asked him, "What good would it do them to poke around here, even if they knew enough to? Bettie Brice has lost every trace of her memory. There's nothing she can say or do that could implicate organized crime any more. All that was twenty years ago."

"But it isn't over yet."

"Isn't it?"

"You're here now."

"Retired."

"Noted."

Invisible fingers seemed to walk up my back, nails leaving little dents in their trek, not hurting, barely annoying, but indicating something was there that I should recognize.

My voice didn't quite sound like me when I half-whispered, "What do you know, Darris?"

A few seconds passed before he said quietly, "Nothing that would hold up in court."

"I didn't ask you that."

"You know how cops are, Jack."

"They're all retirees here."

"Sure. That doesn't stop them thinking. They don't say much, but they think, all right. They aren't under orders here any more than you and I are. But we're still cops and you don't shake all that training and action. We still obey some rules that were never written."

I grinned at him.

He scowled. "What's so funny?"

"How come we'll never be plain old civilians again?"

A faint grin twisted his mouth. "Would you want to?"

When I shook my head, the grin reached his eyes.

Then Kinder reached into his back pocket and brought out a small leather pad. He opened it, wrote a few things in it, took down some personal information related to my police work, then handed me the three sheets to sign.

I frowned at what I saw.

Kinder only smiled and nodded again. "I am authorized by the state of Florida to issue permits to carry a concealed weapon to properly trained personnel. I assume you have your own personal pieces with you."

"A Colt Combat Commander, .45 caliber, a Colt 1911 model and a regulation old fashioned Police Colt .38 revolver. If you want samples of fired slugs, I'll get them to you."

"Nice, but not necessary. However, I'll appreciate the effort. There's a range on the west end of the village."

I studied the ice-blue eyes. "How come you don't trust me, Captain Kinder?"

"They used to call you the Shooter, didn't they?"

"Only the ones who stayed alive."

Kinder's response was to watch me close, a knowing smile on his lips.

"Everything was legal, buddy. Justified and approved," I said.

An eyebrow hiked. "Sure got you one hell of a reputation."

"In case you're wondering about it, I have no intention of improving on it."

A tiny shrug. "Good enough."

"Now, can I ask you something else?"

"Sure."

"Sunset Lodge has got the highest concentration of

cops, firemen and even retired federal law enforcement in the USA. They have equipment here that most cities would envy."

"Anything wrong with any of that?"

I shook my head. "No, but how did it get that way?"

"Sunset Lodge was founded by a wealthy man who had been abducted by the old Dutch Schultz outfit in NYC. Two dedicated police officers tracked down the abductors, rescued the victim after a wild shootout, during which both the cops were wounded. The well-off victim became such a great friend of the police, and, by association, the firemen who had assisted in his rescue, that this place was his gift to Civil Service retirees. If you qualify, cost here is minimal. We are independent and well-funded. Well-protected, too."

"Good enough," I remarked.

"You'll learn more as you go along," he said as he stood up. He handed me a card and told me, "I can be reached through any of these three numbers. Call me for any information."

"Tell me something now."

"Shoot."

I smiled at his choice of word and said, "What's with this Garrison Properties outfit down the road?"

"They've been in business for fifteen years. Some upper-echelon mobsters are among the retirees, but we have no evidence they're any more influential in Garrison than the retired dentists and lawyers. Lately they've been trying to class up their act—expanding their land holdings and putting in major lots, putting up major housing. And trying to capitalize on this place, I'd say."

"But it's been around fifteen years?"

"Yeah, and the clientele pre-existing those new fancy estates isn't very classy. A couple of youth gangs operate out of there and word has it they've been selling drugs."

"Any arrests?"

"Several, but money bailed them out in a hurry."

"That's all?"

"A couple of cars were stolen. One was recovered in Tampa and the other was in a ditch off the road. No damage to the vehicles, but two empty bottles of booze were found on the back seat of one."

"Prints?"

"None that could be identified at this point." He shrugged. "Probably juveniles."

"Well, I'm glad to be here," I said, rising. "Nice to be with the good guys."

He got up, we shook hands, exchanged respectful if wary glances, and Captain Kinder was gone.

I took a two-hour tour of the Sunset Lodge compound until I had the area pretty well defined in my head. I saw four faces I recognized from Manhattan precincts but I didn't call out to them. I passed the S.L. Station House, spotted one old sergeant who'd retired when I got my first promotion and two retirees from the Two-Two and suddenly I was feeling very much at home.

Then I turned at the end of the block and retraced

my path to the building that looked so old but was so new. It was a surprise to see no uniforms showing, but everybody going in and out had that identical cop walk and when you looked at their feet, only two were wearing fancy footwear. The others still held on to their old brogans.

Parking was behind the building and I found a place, backed into it like everyone else did, making a quick getaway easy. Habit is a hard thing to break. When I got out of the car I hadn't gone ten feet when a voice said, "Damn, look who's here!"

Joe Pender had retired as a sergeant when he had put his full time in on the Job. Sergeant was as high as the husky redhead had wanted to go—his pension was adequate and he had made an outside job with another cop, renovating old buildings and renting them, so he wasn't hurting for money.

I said, "Good to see you, pal. I didn't know you'd retired down this way."

As we shook hands he told me, "The wife's doing. She's a real Florida lover. New York got to be too much for her. You moving in?"

"Got a place over on Kenneth Avenue."

"Fancy, man!" he laughed. "That's where the brass have their digs. Got an old commissioner at the far end of the street with a pair of inspectors right beside him."

"They still giving orders?"

"Hell no. This time we have a very democratic club." He paused and nodded toward the building behind him. "Damn, Jack, let's get you in and on the rolls."

"I just got here yesterday."

He wrapped his fingers around my arm and said, "And now is when you get back on duty."

"Duty?"

"Sure. The guys would flip out if they tried to hide their cop background and just be plain civilians. We rotate helping Kinder out on security stuff. No rank, no roll calls, plenty of shooting matches on our own firing ranges."

"Who buys the ammunition?" I asked him.

"We have reloading equipment. All calibers. Even the women get in on this action."

"They safe to keep around?"

"Buddy, there hasn't been a divorce since anybody's been here. This retirement scene is the greatest. Jeannie and I damned near broke up until we moved here. Now we're kissing and hugging all over the place."

And Joe Pender was right. Sunset Lodge was a brand new beginning for a bunch of streetwise old police officers who had brushed the grime of New York and New Jersey off their clothes and took to the shorts and sunshine of Florida.

But they couldn't brush the concept of police action from their station house. The walls still held typed and handwritten memos for member activities and in two locations were official mug shots of current criminals somebody in the big city was forwarding to the clubhouse.

"Like it?" Joe asked me.

"Like I never left home," I remarked.

"Right. Now let's get you signed up. Hell, you even get a badge again. Miniature, of course, but you get five percent off your bills over in the big cities. Just show the tin."

I shook my head and followed him to the reception desk where I became semi-official in this new land of make believe.

I said so long to Joe and went back outside. A half dozen matrons in tennis outfits were squealing like little kids, all anxious to get to the tennis courts for their tee off times or whatever they called it. I had to stare for half a minute before I fully recognized them. The last time I had seen them they were two-hundred-pounders who had to shop in the big and tall ladies' stores, emphasis on the big. Sunset Lodge had turned them into chorus cutie size again. I sure hoped their husbands appreciated them. Damn.

I got back in my car and pulled out of the parking lot.

When a cop went on the street for the first time, he felt like I do now.

Everybody was looking at him. He was being sized up.

The locals would need several takes. *Is he good enough?* they would ask themselves.

The bad guys would know right away. Would he hesitate to kill them? *No. Not this one...not the Shooter....*

I'd thought I had shrugged those reflections off a long time ago, but I guess I hadn't. I drove down to the intersection of my street, slowed down and made the turn.

I'd never had a big dog in my life. Where would you walk one on a leash? How long would you stay out? I circled the block twice without seeing any signs of

Bettie and her greyhound, then finally turned in to my driveway and went up on the porch and eased into a rocker. I sat there for five minutes and it was like waiting for a snake to strike. I was tense all over. My muscles had tightened into a *ready* position, poised, balanced, raring for the go signal.

Then I heard the *yip* and looked to my left. It was a short sound and it had come from a full-throated animal who had spotted something that pleased him and let out a noise to show his appreciation.

Like water spilling from an overflowing jar, the tension went away when I saw Bettie and Tacos come into my direct line of vision and I got up, walked off the porch and waited for her on the sidewalk.

Tacos told her she had company ahead. I heard the nearly muted whine of pleasure.

How the heck would a dog know about us?

So I wouldn't startle her, I said, "It's me, your new neighbor," then added softly, "Jack."

She wore black sunglasses and their blank lenses bore down on me. "I heard all about you a little while ago. The ladies over at the station house keep everyone well informed."

"I know a lot of them."

"So they mentioned. They all like you too. Did you know that?"

"Well, I've never been arrested."

"They don't arrest policemen, do they?" she asked me.

"The heck they don't," I told her.

She was carrying some mail and a few grocery items

in an ornamented wire basket and I slid my fingers under the handle and took it from her. *Was the mail in Braille, or did someone read it to her,* I wondered.

I said, "You handle your dog and I'll carry your groceries up the stairs. First good deed I've done all day."

Slowly, she turned her head and appeared to look down at Tacos. "Strange," she said softly.

"What is?"

"Tacos never moved to stop you from taking my basket from me."

"Should he?"

"He's extremely protective."

"So am I," I said with a grin. "He knows a kindred soul."

I don't know why, with her heightened senses, she couldn't hear my heart beating. My own breath seemed muffled and the muscles in the small of my back had tightened annoyingly. But the oversized greyhound seemed to realize that *something* was happening and his eyes met mine for an instant's inspection, then he tugged at his leash and walked to the porch steps, Bettie following him closely.

At the door she slid the key into the lock, turned the knob, let the dog enter ahead of her and said to me, "Won't you join us for a cold drink, Jack?"

I didn't answer her for a few seconds and she said, "We are neighbors now, you know."

"And you have one oversized greyhound dog with big vampire teeth, if anyone made any moves against you."

"Yes," she agreed quite pleasantly. "That's because he loves me."

The minute delay in my answer almost spoke what was in my mind but hadn't reached my tongue yet. I asked her, "How heavy is Tacos anyway?"

"A hundred and twenty pounds," she told me. "All muscle, extremely bright, but too big to race and not enough dog plumage to stay warm while pulling a sled in heavy snow."

"Where did you get him?"

"He was about to be put down. I rescued him at the track just in time. I wish I could have taken more of the animals, but this one licked my hand and gave me a knowing, pleading look and he became mine and I became his."

"No offense," I said, "but what is a 'knowing' look, when you're blind?"

Without hesitation, she said, "Just that he knew I *was* blind. And that we both needed each other."

I nodded and said a quiet, "Oh. I see."

Her head turned and she looked at me. Behind her dark glasses I knew her eyes had somehow found mine. "Do you really?"

"Really," I murmured.

"Have we met?" she asked abruptly.

"Now why would you ask that? This is my first time here."

Without answering me, she walked to the kitchen. The layout of her place was the same as mine, the two houses built on identical architectural plans.

I heard the refrigerator open and shut and she came back with two glasses of iced tea and handed me one.

Then she sat on the edge of a big ottoman, sipped her tea a moment, and said, "A long time ago I had an accident. That is what I have been told. I have no memory of it at all, nor anything prior to twenty years ago."

"Aren't you interested in finding out any details?"

Bettie shook her head gently. "I've been told I have no living relatives."

"*Somebody* pays your way here."

"Yes," she agreed. "He was the one who…let's say *adopted* me after the accident. He's gone now. Passed away, but he had everything set in motion."

"There were no inquiries about you, over the years?"

"I understand there were. With the mental state I was in, I couldn't care less."

"I'm sorry about that," I said.

Her head turned and she was looking right into my eyes again. It was as though she had echo location like a porpoise and could zero right in on any sound. I wondered if she could hear me blink.

"The body can compensate for loss," she murmured. Then, out of the blue, she asked, "*Say my name.*"

I waited a long moment, took in a deep breath, then quietly said, "Bettie."

Unlike this young woman, I could see, supposedly. I had been trained to observe and fit pieces together so that any puzzle made sense. I could do all that, but this time I was drawing a blank.

She didn't draw a blank, though. "Since you first

spoke to me this morning your voice has had a familiar sound."

"Like how?" I asked.

"Like how I know every sound my dog, Tacos, makes. I know what he is trying to tell me. I recognize his mood, his likes and dislikes. He recognizes mine. Somehow I seem to recognize your speech patterns."

I wanted to blurt it out. I wanted to yell it out loud, but she had a mind that was bent out of shape and I didn't want to put any further dents in it.

I said, "Well Bettie, I'm just an old New York City cop who might spout a lot of idiomatic language or get into some tough street talk, but I don't quite follow your drift here."

There was something very strange about the way she smiled at me. "It will come to me eventually," she said. "Things always do."

Her hand reached out, squeezed my wrist and she asked me, "Can you imagine what it's like, having a new friend?"

I laid my other hand on top of hers and the big dog gave an odd, throaty noise of pleasure.

"Tacos likes you," she told me.

I let out a pleased grunt too. Then I said, carefully, "This may sound strange but…has anybody ever…tried to attack you?"

A frown creased her forehead while she thought, then shook her head. After a few seconds of further thought, she added, "I've never had any trouble with anybody. Everybody in this area knows everybody else.

Everybody here looks after me, or tries to—I don't really need much help.... Why?"

"Well, you're a lovely doll, Miss Brice." I tried to excuse my tone with a tight grin before I remembered she couldn't see it. "I can see why the boys would keep an eye on you."

"But you said *attack*."

"These days," I said, "the courts can label any type of action an attack. A lot of big-mouth wise guys draw some time for sounding off to unprotected women."

"Tacos protects me pretty well," she smiled back. "The only 'big mouth' I've run into lately was a young guy who made a nasty remark..."

"How young?"

"He wasn't some old lecher. Since I couldn't see him I can't describe him, but his voice told the story. Anyway, he never came by again."

"What did you say to him?"

"Nothing. I just gave him what I thought was a dirty look, only maybe he couldn't tell with me in sunglasses."

I made a small probe. "Mind if ask something?'

"No. We're friends."

"Why do you wear them? Sunglasses, I mean. Your eyes are lovely."

She thought about that. "Sometimes I can feel the sun on my eyes—almost as if the glare is bothering me."

"Is it?"

Her head turned and she seemed to look in the direction of my mouth. I felt like kissing her.

She said, "I don't know."

"Explain."

"At the end of the day I...I think I can see a red sunset."

"Oh?"

"The doctors said it was simply a mental reaction. I realized the time of day that it was and expected a red sunset. A sense memory."

"What did you tell them?"

"I wanted to tell them that they were idiots. I saw *something*. And it was a sunset. Nothing definitive, but the colors were there. Something bright and beautiful was shining at me."

"But what did you tell them?" I repeated.

"That I saw a sunset. They made me re-word it to I *thought* I saw a sunset."

"When do you see a doctor again?"

"Never, as far as I'm concerned," she retorted. "I am done with them. I'm blind. All they can say is there is no hope that I'll ever get my eyesight back. So why should I bother with doctors?"

"You giving up?"

"Nope. I'm just going to make do with the best that I have."

"And what is that?"

She thought about that, patting Taco's head until he rubbed his big muzzle against her leg, then she said softly, "I don't remember my past, so my present is always like living in a paper sack, and the future is all blank space."

"That's what you think?"

"Come on, neighbor Jack, what kind of future would I have if I hadn't had a benefactor like my old veterinarian?" She gave me a sudden big smile and added, "How old are you, Jack?"

"I'll never see fifty again."

"I'm almost forty-three."

"You're a kid," I said. "An infant, in this place."

And it was as if something had stabbed her. Her head jerked in my direction and my eyes were suddenly locked into the black lenses shielding her sightless ones and a shudder touched her shoulders.

Then she took a deep breath and released what she was thinking. "What did you say?"

"I said you were a kid."

There was a tautness to her expression, and her eyes seemed to search for me, then whatever she was looking for disappeared from her mental image and she whispered, "Strange."

"What is?"

"Being called a kid," she told me. "Why would I remember that?"

And then *I* remembered it. *I used to call her "kid."* I'd hold her tight and kiss her, tasting all the sweetness that she had and we'd talk about what we'd do when she grew up.

No way would I have recounted any of those conversations to the guys at the station house. Career cops are funny people with the tightest association between partners and other cops, bonds nobody could break. But, hell, I couldn't tell them I was wildly in love with a kid. The old-timers would have run me ragged. When Bettie disappeared in that wild abduction, the ranks closed behind me. I never let them open again.

And now here I was.

And who remembered anymore?

Somebody remembered. I could feel it! Damn it, the years were only a hiatus, a period of waiting, and now it was almost over!

Bettie said, "I have to feed Tacos. Would you like to help me?"

"You need help to feed your dog?"

"I need help to talk to my new neighbor. Your house has been empty ever since I've been here."

I said "Okay, young lady...."

"You did it again."

"What?"

"Called me a 'young lady.' That's worse than 'kid.' "

"You're younger than me," I said.

"Okay, no woman's going to argue with that."

And once again I took her hand in mine and, without realizing it, our fingers intertwined and started speaking a silent language that only special people can understand, and at the top of the stairs Bettie said, "Jack...."

"What?"

"Are you sure?"

"About what?"

Her face turned toward me and she reached up and took off her sunglasses. And there were those eyes. Hazel. Pure hazel. The brown and the green swirled in them. How she found the line of vision to mine was something I didn't know. She was looking at me, watching me, then she let a smile touch her lips.

I snapped my fingers at the greyhound and damned

if that dog didn't smile at me. No tail-wagging, just a daggone smile.

Back in New York City my street was nearly ready for the macadam medical examiner. Nobody had to tell me. I knew the progression of the gravediggers that tore up the entrails of a city and spit them out in some abandoned area that developers would discover and build upon. What was strange was that I didn't care any more. The city was in a state of flux, blowing up like a fat man who had once been skinny and raunchy and enterprising but now was dropping into the mire of his own wealth. He was fat now. He was going to get fatter.

Bettie said, "What are you thinking?"

"You wouldn't want to know, doll."

"Jack...you did it again."

"What?"

"You...you called me 'doll.' "

"That's you all over, baby," I said.

Creases showed at the edges of her eyes and she told me, "It's like hearing an echo. And echoes aren't real....Are they?"

"Something else was there first," I said quietly. "Something real generates echoes...kid."

She gave one of those girl shakes of the head that sent hair spilling across her face and her laugh had that Tinkerbell ring to it.

"Well, let's give my big mutt two cans of his favorite dish and a big bowl of biscuits."

I almost asked her what would come next but she

beat me to the answer first. "Then you can tell me all about *your* past, since I don't seem to have any."

"Police officers are sworn to secrecy," I growled.

"Baloney. They're all writing books about it now. Some of them even made movies about their exploits. You ever know any of those cops, Jack?"

"Eddie Egan," I fired back. "He was a great cop."

"The French Connection episode?"

I nodded, even though she couldn't see me do it. "Among a lot of others."

"What did *you* do, Jack?"

"Routine stuff," I said. "Everything's based on established routine in police work. That's why we almost always nail the bad guy."

"And how was it when you had to leave your job?"

"Until now, it's been lousy."

She let out a little-girl giggle. "What's happened to improve it?"

"I suddenly got a new neighbor. In New York City you never have a new neighbor. They're always the 'people next door' or the person you nod to in the elevator every morning when you leave for work."

She turned around and looked into my eyes. There was no identity recognition, just the crinkly movements at the corner of her mouth so that I knew she was intent upon every word I spoke when she told me, "I don't want to be just...the person next door, Jack."

"Bettie...you're the very special person next door."

Very lightly, her tongue touched her lips and they gleamed with a gentle wetness.

She filled Tacos' bowl with a big helping of his favorite supper and put it on the floor next to the water dish. The dog never moved. There was a peculiarity in his stance that was hard to define. His eyes seemed to be nailed to mine and the tip of his tail gave a minute twitch.

I said, "Bettie, if I don't kiss you I'm going to blow up like I swallowed a grenade."

"Tacos will kill you if you touch me."

"The hell he will," I said and reached out for her, but not too far because she came right into my arms the way she used to and when our mouths touched it was like being smothered in fire of the most pleasurable pain possible. It wasn't a long kiss. It only lasted for the years that had already gone by and absolutely made up for all the wild, crazy wait I'd had to sweat out, never knowing that this would happen.

You can't sustain moments like that for too long. We just stood there, and even when I closed my eyes I knew whom I had kissed, but it was not to be told. Not yet. And Bettie was seeing that same invisible thing too and squeezed my hands gently.

I said, "Tacos didn't try to bite me, kitten."

I looked down at the dog's head, which came up to my hip, and damned if that big old animal wasn't wearing a grin as wide as a mile. His heavy tail gave two mighty thumps against the floor and he let out another of those pleased *yips*.

Very softly, Bettie said, "You've made another very good neighbor, Jack."

I let her words hang in the air, then said, "I'm sorry."

She answered, "Don't be."

"I've just gotten here. One day and look at what has happened. You know what I suddenly feel like? A heel is what I feel like, taking advantage of—"

With her forefinger she touched my lips and said, "Do you know what *I* suddenly feel like?"

There was no way I could answer that question logically.

"I have no memory at all of my younger days. I've been told that I was very pretty and bright and had young men constantly try to get...how do you say it?...next to me."

And as suddenly as she mentioned it, she scowled, a brief flare of memory tugging up some hidden twist of recollection.

"What is it?" I asked.

For a good ten seconds she stood staring off into empty space. It was like a machine grinding away without sound. Wheels were spinning, but not propelling any energy to any of its memory banks.

Blankly, she asked me, "Jack...Jack, what just happened?"

"Something was coming back to you."

She shook her head and wiped her hand across her eyes.

"From before your accident?" I suggested.

The shake of her head was final. "It was nothing. I can't remember any of it. Every once in a while it happens like that."

"Bettie...did that old vet ever get you in to see a psychiatrist when you were with him?"

A shadow of a frown touched her face again and she nodded. "Several times. Why do you ask?"

"Any conclusions on your case?"

"Yes. There has been some sort of brain damage. Nothing life-threatening, but critical enough to cause memory lapse." She stopped abruptly and took her lower lip between her teeth. "Do we have to talk about that?"

Brain damage—two chilling words. The few amnesia cases I'd encountered over my cop years had been psychosomatic. Yet she seemed to be reacting to bits and scraps as I unintentionally jogged those brain cells, damaged or not....

I ran my hand up her forearm and gave her a gentle squeeze. "Of course not, doll. I was just being curious... and stupid."

"No...it's all right. I understand what sort of a curiosity I must be." She smiled again and I wanted to kiss her again but didn't push it.

Then she added, "You're just being a cop, aren't you? Always asking questions." She raised her palm and held it to my cheek. "You're smiling," she told me.

"You're pretty," I told her.

This time she took my hand and drew me into the living room. No one would have ever have thought she was blind. She led me to a large leather-covered chair and eased me into it, then clicked on the TV without any difficulty and sat down on the couch opposite me. The Weather Station came on and we sat watching, or in her case listening, a while. She leaned back against the cushions, stretched her legs out until her toes touched mine and said, "Jack…you are the first real visitor I've ever had in my house."

"That's what neighbors are for."

Even if I had had my eyes closed I would have known she was grinning at me. "What's so funny?" I asked gently.

"It feels so natural, you and me."

"Why do you suppose?"

"I don't know." She paused, then asked, "Do you?"

She couldn't see what I did, but I nodded. And she knew it, too.

"And you're not going to tell me, right?"

I said, "Right. And now it's time to leave. Until tomorrow, anyway."

But she knew I was hiding something. How do women always seem to know these things?

Chapter Five

New York newspapers do a heavy business in Florida. With a big percentage of the population wintering there, visiting another big chunk of their citizens who have already moved to the Sunshine State, the papers keep them well supplied with news from home. On page four of the issue I picked up was a two-column article that I could have skipped over if the name Credentials hadn't popped right out of the text.

Ray Burnwald, the owner of the business, had been shot twice and his personal office and adjacent files had been ransacked along with others that went back some twenty-five years. Others were pulled out of the racks, but hadn't been opened because someone had heard the shots and notified the police. No computers had been taken, possibly because approaching sirens had warned the intruder off. No one seemed to know what he was after. Ray Burnwald was expected to be hospitalized for some time.

Crimes like this are committed for one reason only: money, or some other type of financial gain. Those files were full of paperwork, not valuable artifacts of gold or jewelry that can be cashed out anywhere, but hard copy that dated to when computers were backed up on paper. All those files contained was information and the data couldn't be too critical because it was stored in an easily accessed area.

But was it worth enough to chance getting a murder charge wrapped around someone's neck? That shooting was meant to be a killing one.

I got hold of Sergeant Davy Ross at his new precinct number and asked him to look into the hit on Credentials and find out if Burnwald would be able to talk to me shortly. I sat by the phone for three hours, saw Bettie get picked up by a Sunset Lodge station wagon filled with a half dozen older women, had two pots of coffee and watched an old movie on TV before the call came in.

Davy Ross had worked through the investigating officers on the case and all they had for evidence were the slugs they took out of Ray Burnwald's body. Luckily, he was not in critical condition and would be glad to talk to me at any time. So would the investigating officers. They smelled something interesting going on, even though they had no fingerprints or incidental evidence from the crime scene. Two of Burnwald's current employees, one of whom was in charge of the filing system, had no idea what the intruder was after, though he did mention that three of the folders seemed to have been more thoroughly perused than all the others. But on a check with duplicate information, nothing was missing.

I asked Davy if he had the dates covered by those three folders and when he checked his notes he gave me the year, month and weeks of my requests.

Over the phone Davy asked, "Watcha got on this deal, Jack?"

"Nothing yet."

"But you're thinking something."

"Damn right, Davy, but let me check it out a little further. I don't want to drop any problems on the guys processing this. Let me know if you get a make on those slugs they took out of Burnwald."

"You got it, buddy. Anything else I can do?"

"Not yet. Soon, maybe."

"The guys want to know how you're doing."

"I'm hanging in there. How's the street?"

"The old lady's still hanging out the window on her pillow."

"She was supposed to go to Elizabeth."

"Her daughter got sick. She's due to come today, they tell me."

"Won't they ever let that street die a decent death?"

"Crazy. You take care, Jack. By the way, you need any more .45 ammo?"

"We get it all for free down here. Besides, nobody's around to shoot."

Davy let out a chuckle, said so long and hung up.

I looked at the notes I had scratched on my lap pad. The dates of the most "perused" files were right before Bettie had been abducted.

And there was that word again. *Abducted.* Killing her would have been easier.

And what were they looking for in the old Credentials files? Nothing seemed to be missing.

Three folders had been given more than a casual inspection.

And those three folders were dated just before the hit on Bettie.

Had something alerted Bettie to information in those files?

Had Bettie removed the pertinent items herself, most likely to give to me?

If so, Bettie had no memory at all about the event.

Damn!

Psychiatrists probe minds. They don't operate. They don't give physical therapy. They probe minds and try to make sense out of what's there. Sometimes it works. They say bartenders are great at that too because their "patients" get bent out of shape with booze and hand the guy behind the bar all kinds of gibberish he has to sort out to keep the gibberish from turning into a bar brawl. Cops have to play the same game to keep a lot of loudmouths from doing jail time and for being able to recognize the little mental slips and omissions the bad guys fabricate to ease out of an arrest.

This job was not something we really studied at the Academy. It was strictly street smarts.

I heard back from Davy Ross a few hours later. I recognized his voice, said, "Hi, buddy. What do you have?"

"Forget any ID on those Burnwald slugs. They didn't match any in the ID files, but photos of them are at hand. Most likely the shooter has already dropped the gun in the river and there are no witnesses who saw anyone make an entrance into the Credentials offices."

I nodded into the phone. "Thought it would be that way."

"What have you got in your mind, Jack?"

"Nothing I can put into words, pal. I'll be in touch when I can."

"Roger and out, Captain," he said, then added with a laugh. "That's G.I. talk, remember?"

"How could I forget?" I told him.

Before I could hang up, he said, "Hey, Jack!"

"Yeah?"

"Damn near forgot to tell you. I just saw old Bessie O'Brian, when her daughter picked her up. She told me something funny."

"Like what?"

"She said she saw a guy wandering around that dead old street…reminded her of Bucky Mohler, who used to live down from her. You remember *that* piece of work, don't you?"

"Sure, Davy—and I remember the Blue Uptowners nailing Bucky with a stolen car. Mashed the hell out of him."

"Well, you know old Bessie. Whatever happened on that street, she'd know about."

"Yeah, she always was a reliable old bird, only this time she has to be off the track."

"You so sure?"

"Bucky's wallet and a dry cleaner's ticket were in his pocket. Bloodstained, but readable."

"Maybe, Jack. But even his family couldn't identify Bucky, at the morgue. And old Bessie says she saw him."

"Bessie's older than dirt, Davy."

"So are we, Jack. So are we…."

*

She knew I'd be coming over there.

So did her dog. When my hand turned the doorknob, I heard Tacos' soft yip and Bettie's head turned and her smile reached between the two houses and she waved.

She wasn't wearing her sunglasses, and somehow her pupils followed me down the steps and across to her porch. When I reached her she held up her hand the way she used to twenty years ago and when I kissed it her eyebrows gave a minute twitch and nobody had to remind me that this was an unconscious act of remembrance. I had kissed her hand many times in the past, but not where somebody could see me do it. Big cops never did that sort of thing to young ladies. To their mothers, maybe, or grandmothers, but not to a beautiful, sensuous doll.

Cops sure had a lot to learn.

I pulled up another rocker and sat down beside her. I didn't try to be surreptitious with my question, but something had to jar her recognition facilities and I said, "You used to work at a place called Credentials, didn't you?"

"Why..." Her mouth creased and she paused. "That sounds a little bit familiar. I think. Remember, I only *think*."

"Good enough."

"Is it important?"

Now was the time I had to sink the barb in. I told her, "The man who owns Credentials was shot and the files ransacked. He was injured, but he's alive. His name was Ray Burnwald."

"Mr. Burnwald!" she blurted out, almost painfully. The skin of her face paled.

"Did you know him?"

"I...I...don't remember. It seems like...."

"What?"

"The name...I've heard it before." She looked at me, not seeing me, but as if she were.

"Would it bother you if I gave you some more information?" I asked her gently.

"No, please."

I said, "You worked on computers at Credentials. Your job was data management."

Bettie seemed to mouth the words, a small frown tensing her lips. "Data management," she repeated quietly. "Mr. Burnwald was...nice."

And that was all I got.

But it was a start.

Again, that look. She was seeing me without seeing me. Her pupils were locked directly on mine and there was a vague expression in them. It lasted for about five seconds, then went back to non-recognition again.

That was a start, too.

Her mood seemed to impart itself to the greyhound. He paused in the middle of a big yawn that showed a mouthful of huge teeth, and his head moved a few inches to scan the both of us, wondering what made this visit so intense.

I reached over, squeezed her arm and said, "How about us three taking a drive? It's a beautiful day and..."

"But I can't see it, Jack."

"So I'll describe it to you and you can smell the flowers. Tacos can bark at passing cars."

"Tacos doesn't do that," she said.

"Good. Now let's go."

The greyhound hopped into the back seat, happy to have the space all to himself, with the window cracked down so he could smell the flowers too. We drove through the center of the village and friends of Bettie called out to her and waved. Two of my old buddies made some odd grimaces when they saw me out with my blind, but very striking, lady friend.

Two blocks up the musical bells of an ice cream truck rolled out its national theme song. I asked Bettie if she wanted a cone and she shook her head. "Those boys on those trucks are too fresh."

"What did they do?"

"I was walking the dog and they whistled and made pretty rude remarks."

"What were you wearing?"

"Halter top and shorts. It's what all the girls wear."

"Bettie," I said, "you are not built like all the other girls. With your shape in shorts, kid, you're a stone killer."

"Stone killer?"

"Absolutely. You can be a danger to the younger population."

Directly ahead was the entrance to Garrison Properties and this time there was a uniformed guard at the small building. He came out with a clipboard, took down my New York license plate numbers and asked if he could help me.

"Just want to look at some properties," I told him.

"The Garrison office is right at the center of the village. You can't miss it."

I told him thanks and drove up the road.

I could see what Darris Kinder meant when he said what the Garrison group was up to, with their estates across the way and allying themselves geographically to Sunset Lodge to entice future buyers. Stakes marked out generous areas for ownership and as I drove closer to the buildings of the village, the houses went from typical Florida-style residential homes with two- or three-bedroom capacities to enormous and expensive multi-story buildings with expensive foreign and domestic vehicles parked in tree-shaded driveways.

Bettie broke the long silent moment with, "What are you looking at, Jack?"

"Big money," I told her. "This bunch in Garrison is loaded with the green."

"It's so quiet."

"Money buys that, too," I reminded her.

"Sunset Lodge isn't like that at all."

"You ever know any rich cops or firemen?"

She shook her head and laughed. "But I don't know anybody, anymore. Do *you* know any rich ones?"

"Only if they went into the movies or hit a national jackpot," I said, not mentioning the handful of bent ones I'd come across. Then I added, "Well there aren't any cops or firemen out this way. Right from here I can see three mansions that must've cost in the two-million dollar range to build. Off to the right there's one hell of a golf course with one hell of a clubhouse on it."

"Who's playing on it?"

"Nobody," I informed her. "It's probably too hot for the big shot tourists."

There was a crossroad just ahead of me with a stop sign facing us and I slowed down to let two ice cream trucks go by. There were no jingling bells ringing out on this hallowed ground. They were following the road that led to the boat basin to peddle the ice cream to the fishermen. When I told that to Bettie she let out a soft laugh and said, "Good luck to them, then. The fishermen at Sunset all drink beer."

She was right. Sunset Lodge was where the great masses went.

So why would anybody want to edge in on Sunset's popularity? You would think the mob element Garrison catered to would want to be anywhere but next door to a bunch of retired law enforcement. Or were they just thumbing their nose?

"What're you thinking?" Bettie asked.

"Old-time cop thoughts," I answered.

"You people are weird," she giggled.

Before she could close her mouth I leaned over and kissed her. Her hand lay beside my leg and she gave my knee a gentle squeeze. She used to do that back in the days long ago. It was her way of saying thanks. Something in her mind hadn't been destroyed after all. Those involuntary reflexes seemed to work on their own. But squeezing my leg wasn't a true involuntary reflex. Her head suddenly turned and she was looking straight at the side of my face and I knew she was smiling. Then she leaned over and lightly brushed her mouth across my cheek.

So I squeezed her leg. Soft and easy. I could say thanks too.

There were commercial buildings waiting for occupancy and several stores at full development, but not teeming with shoppers. Nor were there many people on the sidewalks. A car lot one block off the main road held about thirty high-priced vehicles and only two men were looking at the mechanical marvels.

This town wasn't dying, it just hadn't come alive yet. Everything was here, waiting for its birth, but the critical time hadn't arrived yet. It was coming, but it had a way to go.

"You want to stop for anything?" I asked Bettie.

"Can I let Tacos out?"

"Sure. There's a big empty lot up ahead."

I parked while she let the dog walk and when he finished his business, she started back to the car then tripped over something. The dog picked it up and carried it between his teeth.

I said, "I think Tacos made a find...."

Bettie said, "*Now* what's he got?"

"Not a bone."

I held out my hand and the dog dropped a well-used little gadget in my hand. I didn't tell his mistress it was an expensive hand-carved miniature ivory pipe, the sort rich little slobs liked to tote around to puff on weed or hash. This one was a slinky little off-white dame designed to have a glowing red head. At night these dark, empty fields made great playgrounds. And there should be plenty of young rich slobs around to have some crazy games.

I said, "A kid's toy."

"Oh? What kind?"

"A bubble pipe," I lied.

"The hell it is," she contradicted me softly. "Let me feel it."

I dropped it in her palm and watched the way she rolled it around before handing it back to me.

I said, "So?"

"Carved horn or ivory, probably the latter. The engravings are still fairly sharp-edged, so it isn't antique, is it?"

"No."

"It's supposed to be a woman, isn't it? With a curvy figure?"

"Not as curvy as yours."

She sniffed it. "Smells like hash."

"You got it, doll. It's not even an interim action any more. It becomes a dependency, but an affordable one. If you got wealthy patrons, you got it made. If not, you can steal, rob or merchandise the junk until you get slapped into a jail cell." Then I put in, "Or killed. I almost forgot the tag line. Captain Kinder says, despite the money clientele coming in, some youth gangs still operate out of here. Maybe one of those punks dropped that pipe."

This time Bettie wasn't looking toward my face. She

was staring straight ahead watching a mental picture flash through her mind. I kept quiet, letting her focus on her thoughts, wondering what direction it was taking.

She finally said, "*Credentials*," and her right hand was squeezed into a tight fist. She draped one arm over the back of the car seat and let Tacos lick her skin.

I nudged her memory and softly said, "Credentials," until her head bobbed in acknowledgment and she said, "There was an employee there. A young man. *He* had a pipe like that. I can even remember…remember what it smelled like."

"Who, Bettie? What was the young man's name?"

She shook her head. The big black cloud had come over her again.

"I don't know," she murmured.

I had handled enough blackout cases who were behind bars for some wild criminal activity and watched them dissolve into total ignorance under pressure. You had to let it alone until some semblance of memory came back and they were able to talk about it. It could be frustrating as hell, but you were the cop and you stayed with it until the door opened on their thoughts and you got another little piece that made sense.

I cut over to the main thoroughfare and steered to the entrance gate. On the way out there was no query by the guard, just a short wave, then we were on the highway again. In the back of the car the greyhound knew we were going home and gave out a cheery yip to tell us about it.

At the house I walked Bettie up the steps, my arm

around her waist. She wanted me to stay for supper. I begged off, telling her I had a lot of work to catch up on, but I'd see her later.

This time she smiled gently, licked her lips and held her face up to mine.

I said, "Somebody might be watching."

"Nobody's around, Jack. Tacos would have seen them if there were."

So what's an old cop to do?

Her mouth was warm and damp and quivering and things began happening to me so that I untangled myself gently. She knew what I was feeling. She let me go. Her eyes still had that blankness, but she knew.

When Tacos went in the front door ahead of her, I went down the steps and across to my house. My notebook was on the end table beside the big chair and when I'd made myself comfortable, I uncapped my ballpoint pen and started writing down events of the day with my own little interpretations of them.

I took the ivory pipe, wrapped it in a couple of tissues and put it on the shelf in the secret cabinet with my guns. I wasn't concerned with prints on the surface. The carved engravings were too intricate to have picked up any full impressions. But whoever had made the piece might have left an identification in his own fancy artwork.

A half hour later I caught Davy Ross as he was coming off duty and asked him who was handling identifying unusual criminal artifacts and he gave me the phone number and office address of the right department and I dialed it into the phone. It was after office hours, but cops with a scientific bent don't hold to absolute schedules.

The officer that answered the phone the squad used to make a joke out of because he came from a wealthy family, had two degrees from major universities and all he had ever wanted was to be a cop. He worked and studied his way to sergeant, had a chest full of awards he was embarrassed to wear because he thought unusual heroics in enforcing the law was what he had been hired for. Then finally, when he provided some super cop with super rank certain critical scientific evidence that resulted in some grand busts, he was installed in the slot he had always wanted. His name was Paul Burke and he was glad to hear from me.

I said, "Hi Paul, Jack Stang from…"

"Come on, Jack, you're still a legend around here. What's going on?"

"I found what looks to be a finely tooled ivory hash pipe. It may have some significance, but it doesn't appear to be the kind just any punk would have."

"Intricate carvings?"

"Very."

"Can you send it up here FedEx?"

"Consider it shipped. You still at the same location?"

"Right between the microscopes and the test tubes."

"No street work anymore?"

"Oh, I wangle that in when I can. Shot me a robber last week. Just a nick, but it sure scared the hell out of him."

"What were you aiming for?"

"The spot right where I hit him," he told me. "Hell, I didn't want to take him down permanently."

"Pal, you're an oddball cop, you know that?"

"Sure I do. Did you know I'm up for a promotion?"

"Great!"

"I won't take it unless I can stay right here."

After a few seconds I asked, "What do you do with all your dough, Paul?"

"Send decent kids to college who couldn't afford it otherwise. Two of them are going into the Academy this year."

"You are some recruiter, buddy."

"Get that pipe up to me fast, okay?"

"You got it," I said.

With FedEx you make one phone call and they have it on the way in no time. Not every change has been for the worse.

Just most of them.

It's odd to watch a blind person prepare supper.

You expect them to break a dish or shake in something that doesn't belong there or not find the filter basket with a spoonful of coffee and spill it all over the counter. The TV was on the evening news but I wasn't bothering to watch it. Bettie's body was in beautiful motion, the way I had always thought it would be. There was grace in every movement and whatever she did had deliberate thought behind it.

I sat across the table and she knew I was studying her, watching every move she made and storing it away in my memory banks. I didn't have to tell her. She knew. When she cleared away the supper plates and set a fat piece of fresh apple pie in front of me, she asked me, "Jack…how did this all happen?"

"Kismet," I said.

"Oh? Simple fate?"

"Not so simple."

"You're thinking something else, aren't you?"

"Yes."

"What?"

"It *had* to happen."

"Why?"

"Kismet," I repeated.

Outside, the sun was setting in the west and some shore birds were cutting streaks through the darkening sky. Bettie and I rocked in unison in the big wicker-backed chairs and my mind was a million miles away from the cacophony of sounds that made New York City the Big Apple. It was a great nickname until you remembered that people took bites out of big apples and if one of those bites nipped your rear end, it shouldn't be a total surprise.

Darris Kinder's Batman car turned the corner, pulled up in front of Bettie's house and he cut the engine. He came out of the vehicle, took a casual look around the area and walked up to the porch.

I stood up and said, "Captain, it's good to see you. What's happening?"

"Got to make sure all our new guests are comfortable."

"Can't you tell?"

Kinder looked at the two of us and grinned. "Oh, yeah. I can see that."

I pulled over another rocker and said, "Have a seat. This is the first time we've had any real company."

His face had a bland expression, but I had seen bland expressions before and the look I gave him said I got the implication of what he was thinking.

"It's a quiet night," I offered.

He nodded in agreement. "We've always had quiet nights," he said, but there seemed to be some almost-silent emphasis on the word "quiet."

He went on: "The guys at the Station House had a meeting earlier. They want to get you 'initiated.' "

"I already signed up."

"That's not being initiated."

"Darris, it's great to be here, but I'm not the 'joiner' type. You know?"

"Sure, but tell your old buddies that, not me.... Say, you remember Pudgy Gillespie, don't you?"

"From the thirty-second? Yeah."

"Well, he's thinking of moving down here." Darris passed me a sheet of small notepaper. "Here's his number. Give him a call."

His voice was friendly and bland, but there was a funny tone in it and I nodded and said, "Sure thing, I'll get him later."

When he left, Kinder looked back at me for a quick second and his eyes were telling me something that Bettie couldn't see.

But Bettie had been blind for a long time. Sight wasn't a total necessity for her vision any longer. There were other ways she could see, and when Kinder drove off Bettie very quietly asked, "What was that all about, Jack?"

Her inquiry was so loaded with suggestion that I couldn't lie to her. "Something's happening," I told her.

"What?" she demanded.

"It's a cop thing, doll."

"I don't understand."

"Because you're not a cop."

"Are you?"

"I was."

"...Can you tell me?"

"I can."

"Will you?"

So you love the girl. She's old enough to be a woman but she was born twenty years ago, even if she's forty-something, so she's a girl, who's been through her own hell. She's still in it, but beginning to see the light shining through the murk. You've kissed her and tasted her and you're in total love with her and now she wants to be more a part of you than ever before.

I said, "I will."

"Then tell me."

"Something happened at Credentials where you worked. It was a computer business, so it had to do with the machinery you operated there. Computers, can you remember that? Ray Burnwald was your boss."

"Poor Mr. Burnwald. You said he was...injured?"

"Yes. He's recovering."

"Mr. Burnwald was nice."

"Do you remember your job there?"

For thirty seconds I got a blank stare, then she squinted her sightless eyes, seeing into a past a long time ago. She waited a little longer and said, "Fission."

"What?"

"Fission," she repeated. "Does that…mean anything to you, Jack?"

Silently, I mouthed a string of words that had nothing to do with my thoughts because things suddenly started to make a little bit of sense if you consider all the possible potential of that single word.

FISSION.

Nuclear devastation.

And only a retired cop and a blind beauty to stop it.

Chapter Six

Don't mess with a bunch of pros.

They may have been low-paid cops, but they had been trained and were experienced and had gone through the muck and mire of the defects of society and been shot at and sometimes hit and sometimes killed and when they had something to contribute to the general welfare of the society they had protected for so long, you had damn well better listen to them.

Pudgy Gillespie, newly retired sergeant, who had gotten hit twice when he stopped a bank robbery, said, "Jack, I got hold of some information I think you've been looking for."

"Oh?" I said to the voice on the phone.

"Bennie Orbach was released from prison four months ago," Pudgy said. "He served out all those years for that attempted hijacking of that army truck that was transporting atomic materials to a new location. You remember that?"

That word *atomic* made my neck tingle.

I nodded, then said, "That truck was a dummy, wasn't it? The real one got through."

"The hell it was a dummy. That story came out only when it was found empty."

"A cover-up," I said.

"Like you can't believe. All personnel connected to

that affair were assigned to scattered outposts, kept from making contact until everything quieted down or they died, and until now certain Washington agencies have sat on this thing like it was Fort Knox's gold hoard."

I waited.

When he had his breath back, Pudgy added, "Benny Orbach went into deep cover as soon as he hit the street. He totally disappeared, never even attempting to contact his parole officer, but a couple of our hot shot trackers from downtown picked up a thread of information and followed it up."

"They located Benny?"

"No, they found what was left of his body. Somebody had really worked him over and whatever he was holding out, he spilled. Nobody could have kept quiet with the kind of sticking he was given. It was almost like a living autopsy."

"Damn," I spit out.

"But they missed something," Pudgy said. "They never found his personal stash."

I squinted silently at that.

Pudgy told me, "You know how the cons hide their most necessary items, like narcotics?"

With the way prison shakedowns are held, I couldn't imagine any way any con could hold out anything. After a few seconds I suggested, "You referring to rectal implants?"

"Exactly."

"Hell, Pudgy, they would have found that before he was released. Their inspections are…"

"Come on, Jack. He was *released.* He used the

implant *after* he got out. Whoever nailed him never even thought of that."

"You don't think he wouldn't have talked, being carved up like that?"

Pudgy said solemnly, "One of our medics said pain and fear could have distorted his memory functions. In other words, he went out of his noodle."

"Cut to the chase, Pudgy."

"The condom up his ass had a note in it, only the thing leaked…but one word was still decipherable. It said Credentials."

"Shit."

"So to speak. Also a number, Jack: 4428."

"How did you connect Credentials to me, Pudge?"

"I had lunch with Davy Ross the other day and he mentioned you, and Credentials came up. Almost like an afterthought with him."

"But not with you," I said.

"You know old cops, Jack. That's why I'm passing it on. Maybe you can add it up."

"Some things are standing tall enough to leave a shadow, pal."

"Got you."

When I hung up I stared at the phone. There was no way I could get any information from a government agency, even if I knew which one to tap. They ran their own railroad and didn't share the engineer's seat with anybody else; but something big had gone down and now it was coming back up again.

Benny Orbach had stolen a shipment of atomic material. It had been offloaded before the truck was found.

The load had to be put in a specially adapted vehicle.

It would have to be stored somewhere safe. No radiation emissions.

Who would be the ultimate purchaser?

Credentials was not a storage area...What was *it* used for?

What did 4428 mean?

There was an ambiguous side to the death of Benny Orbach—most likely any investigators would assume that the word "Credentials" in Benny's implant would refer to identification in a drug deal.

But cops have their own sources of information too. Mine was a library where a cheery-voiced young lady was happy to research the affair of the hijacked Army vehicle that was transporting atomic material.

It only took her a minute on the computer to run it down and she told me the value of the shipment was over five hundred million dollars. *Back then.* What would it be worth now, in a world of terrorists backed by oil-rich sugar daddies?

The atomic material was never recovered and supposition was that the robbery never even happened.

Typical government subterfuge.

All this, now that my blind Bettie had dredged a deadly word from her fractured memory: *fission*.

Bettie was letting her dog lick her ice cream cone when I crossed over to her porch.

I said, "That healthy, doll?"

"He won't get sick," she laughed.

Down the street I heard the bells from the ice cream

truck. "I thought you didn't like those fresh kids."

"This one was new," she told me. "Tacos didn't even growl at him. Can I get you anything?"

"I'm fine. I came over to ask you something."

"Oh?"

"When you were at Credentials…"

"Jack, I can't remember those things. Sometimes I get a fuzzy picture, but I can't make out what it is."

"Okay. Does the number forty-four-twenty-eight mean anything to you?"

Her facial expression was blank and she shook her head. "Should it?"

"I don't know. There's no prefix, so it isn't a phone number." Then I gave it further thought and asked, "A file number?"

No use. She stared at me and shook her head.

"Listen, I have to check something out. Something out of town."

"Kind of used to having you around, Jack."

"Stay that way."

And I kissed her. And she kissed me.

I don't know if it helped her remember anything, but parts of me beside my memory bank were getting stimulated, all right.

"Why don't we leave Tacos down here with the ice cream," she said, "and go upstairs and…jog my memory."

"Listen, doll—you've only known me since—"

"Forever."

She took my hand and the blind led the blinded up the stairs into the bedroom. A shorts and halter top fell to the floor and she crawled up on the bed and onto her back and opened her arms and herself to me.

Every peak and valley of her long-legged body was exactly as my dreams had replayed them over too many years. I started out gentle but she urged me on, demanded I let all of the pent-up passion out and into her....

Forever, she'd said.

I wasn't sure that would be long enough.

That evening I drove to the airport and left for New York. It was a direct flight and I got in early enough to go to the hospital where Ray Burnwald was being treated, identified myself to the uniformed officer at the door and he told me Burnwald was able to speak, but not for long.

When I went in Ray heard the door snick shut and opened his eyes. There was apprehension there for a moment, then the man in the hospital bed recognized me.

"I was shot," he whispered.

He looked pale and drawn but wasn't hooked up to an IV or any other life support. He was on the mend, all right.

I nodded. "I know."

"I didn't see who did it," he added. "I don't know why they did it, either."

"The files that were disturbed—was there anything missing?"

"They were over twenty years old, Captain Stang. We couldn't tell."

"What was the nature of the files?"

He shook his head, bewildered and frustrated. "Just messages to and from our clients."

"Standard language?"

"Sometimes coded, but that was just how they handled their business affairs. We had no knowledge of what it meant." He smiled gently and said, "We are really just a transmission service."

"I see. Has anyone asked for copies of those files?"

"They were over twenty years old," Burnwald repeated.

I asked him, "Could you possibly remember who owned those files, or who had access to them?"

"Bettie…Bettie was the only one who might know… but she's dead."

I let the comment hang, but Burnwald didn't notice.

Then, suddenly, he raised his hand and said, "Wait."

I let him take his time. He was reaching back twenty years for something that had just come to him. When he finally had it in perspective he told me, "The client paid in advance. He wanted service for twenty-five years."

"That's a long time."

"That's why it made an impression. That's why I remembered…."

"He pay by check?"

Burnwald shook his head. "No. He gave me cash. I put it in a manila envelope and had Bettie deposit it right away. It was a very sizable amount."

"And you gave him a receipt?"

"No. He didn't want one. I tried to tell him it was a

tax-deductible transaction, but he refused. I…didn't try to push it any further. The customer is always right, you know."

"Did Bettie see him?"

Burnwald thought a moment, then nodded. His eyes had the clarity of vivid memory. "Yes. I called her in to give her the money in the large envelope." He bit on his lower lip and his eyes watered. "She was a nice girl. It was too bad…what happened to her."

I had been there too long. He was getting tired and twice he winced in pain.

So we shook hands gently and I went on outside. Halfway down the corridor, a doctor was walking up, consulting a chart in his hands. I said to the uniformed officer at the door, "Nobody's been here, okay?"

He got the drift right away and said, "Okay, Captain."

It was nice to have a reputation. Being nicknamed the Shooter leaves a mark on everybody's mind.

On the flight back I kept thinking about that one thing Burnwald had told me. He couldn't remember the man, but paying in advance for twenty-five years worth of service was a damned unusual request. What was supposed to happen at that time? Who would get the information? And what was the information about?

There was another factor running right along with this one. A five hundred million dollar shipment of government-owned atomic material was missing.

And a blind girl whose memory was filling in a thousand-piece jigsaw one puzzle piece at a time could be the key to everything. They had tried to kill her once but the attempt had failed. It was twenty years later, but could she still be recognized? Would she still be slated for a kill?

So I said to myself, screw the details and start off with the kidnapping. Why was Bettie the target back then? Could Bettie possibly have recognized the man for somebody other than who he was pretending to be?

When we were together, she'd been an avid reader of newspapers, had two national news magazines delivered to her home and for mental excitement attended court cases of nefarious criminals. I went with her twice, but those things were pretty damn dull after getting your hands dirty in making an arrest on those slobs.

I was back to being the barroom psychiatrist again. You didn't need a college degree for that. Experience would do nicely, with some cop smarts on the side.

When I got my car out of the parking area beside the airport I drove directly home. The lights in Bettie's house were on, so I parked in my carport and walked up the stairs of her porch. I heard Tacos sound off with a happy yip and when Bettie opened the door she held her arms out and gave me a big squeeze.

And all those years of not having her were suddenly wiped away again. She was more charmingly beautiful than ever, still smelling of little-girl freshness and wasn't at all surprised when I kissed her lightly.

But lightly wasn't what she wanted. There was an excited quivering to her, almost a sparkle in her sightless eyes and she said, "I remembered you, Jack! It was like waking from sleep when you have a great dream, but can only recall it for a second."

I waited a long moment and she continued, "It was from a long time ago! We were young!"

"I was never young, Bettie."

"It *was* you, wasn't it?"

"Would you want it to be?"

"Oh, yes," she said very softly.

Tacos' tail thumped the floor. If I had a tail, I would have thumped it too.

When all the exuberance had settled down, I sat next to her on the sofa and recounted my visit with her old boss. With the medical details out of the way, I eased into his telling me about the customer who bought twenty-five years of service in advance.

And that got a reaction. It had come from some-place way back in her mind and opened a mental door she thought had been shut forever. Her shoulders made a sudden twitch and her whole body tensed, then she said barely audibly, "He paid in cash."

I waited without speaking.

"He...I had seen him before." Her eyes were staring at the other side of the room. "He was...*wrong*."

"How was he 'wrong,' Bettie?"

"He was bad."

"You are sure of that?"

"They didn't convict him." She frowned, her fore-head wrinkling.

I knew now what was going through her mind. She had seen the guy in one of those court cases she enjoyed attending. He had been up on charges and had not been convicted, but the D.A. had leveled some pretty heavy evidence on him, enough to put in her mind that he was "wrong."

Trying to sift this event out without a photo ID of the guy would be nearly impossible. But at least it was a start.

I asked her, "Do you remember working at Credentials at all?"

Hesitatingly, she replied, "I think so."

"What was it like?"

She pursed her lips and shook her head. "Like a dream."

Then I took a wild swing at a badly pitched ball and said softly, "Remember when you looked at that man's files?"

Her answer was a strange, jerky nod. "There were odd symbols and numbers. Pages of them." Then she turned and gave me one of those sightless stares and said, "Where is...Oak Ridge?"

I took a deep breath. Oak Ridge was the site of a nuclear development installation a long time ago. She didn't notice my reaction and went on, "There was something else..."

"What?"

I saw that familiar blank expression again.

"I don't know," she said. That special moment had disappeared, but it had lasted longer than former episodes and if I played it right her memory might spark another bright moment.

Might. Maybe. Foggy words you couldn't depend upon.

From out of nowhere, I said, "Where are those files now, Bettie?"

With a small smile and a solemn tone she said, "I took them."

"Why?"

"That man was…bad."

"Yes?" I encouraged her.

"I opened a sealed envelope. I saw the words…" And she paused, frowned deeply and said quietly, " 'Expected mass destruction potential,' then a large number and…" She drifted off into total silence, looking straight across the room, seeing nothing at all. She turned back to me, her beautiful face taut with anxiety.

She said to me, "Jack…what happened to me just then?"

"You were returning to normal. You damn near made it."

"My memory…?"

"A little bit of it was showing."

"Do you think…?"

"We'll take it easy," I interrupted her.

"What did I say?" Sudden interest was showing on her face.

I was taking a chance, but I went ahead anyway. "You mentioned expected mass destruction potential."

"I did!"

"You did," I repeated.

"Mass destruction," she said. "I've heard that on the news."

"Often, probably," I said. "It's a common enough

expression today. The civilized world is shaking in its boots, hoping the more aggressive nations don't get weapons to cause it."

I was watching her closely now. Her mind was trying to break through its barrier and tell her something. "What else?" she asked me.

"You opened an envelope and read it there."

She frowned and nodded.

I added, "Where is the envelope, Bettie?"

She didn't answer immediately. She was like a computer whose electronics were on a search pattern, making thousands of contacts a second to find the answer to a query the operator typed in. A minute passed, then another. They seemed like hours. Then she simply shook her head and let her unseeing eyes stare at me. "I don't know."

"You hid it," I said bluntly.

Her answer was a quiet, "Yes."

"Good!"

"But...I don't remember where."

When you interrogate a crime suspect you don't have to do it all at once. Fear and aggravating circumstance can block his memory, so you give the suspect a chance to recover the information you want. He may try to disguise it, but the interrogator is an expert and can spot the opening when it appears, and then he's up to bat and the right pitch will come along and the ball will go over the fence. Bettie wasn't a crime suspect, but the situation was damn near identical.

Out of the blue she said, "Jack...tell me about us."

"Us?"

"Before you came here. It didn't just 'happen,' did it?"

When I said no she noticed the quietness in my voice and didn't say a word. She was waiting for me to explain another part of her life that had been taken from her. She was rational, she could think, she could reason, but would she be able to comprehend the details of the past without losing any of the progress she had made?

Now the ball was in my court.

I said, "Twenty years ago you and I were in love. We were going to get married."

Damn...she was smiling!

I felt a little bit nervous. She was waiting so I continued. "At work you uncovered something in the files that was so important to the public welfare that you pulled it out and carried it home with you. You knew I was a cop and planned to show it to me. Unfortunately, I figure the guy who had left that information at Credentials returned, discovered what had happened and the finger led right to you. He employed some hired killers to wipe you out...after snatching you and retrieving those files. It had to be a quick move, simple torture would have made you talk, then your body would have been disposed of."

Bettie's face didn't show any deep concern at all. She was digesting the details and studying them; then she asked me, "What happened?"

"Good neighbors. They suspected what was happening. Deliveries of rugs don't happen at that time of night. Somebody notified 911, the police responded and a squad car came immediately. The chase went on until the truck crashed, went over the bridge and into the river. Somehow you survived by grabbing hold of an inflated inner tube that was in the truck."

"And?"

"You know the rest. The good veterinarian in Staten Island rescued you. He prepared for your future. His son, your adopted brother, carried the doc's wishes out into the present. And here you are."

"*We* are," she told me very quietly. Tacos' tail thumped the floor again and just as softly as her first remark, she asked me, "Jack, are you in love with me?"

"Incredibly so," I said. "Now, may I ask *you* something?"

I didn't have to repeat her question at all.

She simply said, "Incredibly so."

We both had our eyes closed when I kissed her. We were blind but all-seeing and now we had the world in our hands.

At least for the moment. It was like surviving the monstrous blast of an A-bomb.

And that thought put me right back on the track again. Somewhere, secreted away, was a hoard of nuclear material that could blast a major city wide apart.

It was time to start calling in favors. When I got back to my house the first one went to NYPD police tech Paul Burke.

He told me that enriched uranium the size of a football could be designed to wipe out a vast area.

With the right secondary devices incorporated into the main device, subsequent devastation could cause intense radiation injury that could wipe out an entire country. In some arenas of scientific speculation, it was considered possible to eliminate nearly all of the world's population.

"Except for the small group who planned to do the repopulating," I suggested.

"That would be the general idea."

"Feasible?" I asked.

"If you want to speculate," he said. "There are always wise guys like cops who seem to bust things up."

"Quit being so damned cheerful, Paul."

"Sure," he said. "Now, what do you *really* need?"

"That nuclear material was probably enriched uranium. It has to be stored someplace. It had to have been transported in a secure manner with no radiation leakage and that would be in a mobile compartment inside the truck. Now, the truck was found empty. The cargo, being mechanically mobile, was taken in another vehicle and brought to a secure location. What would that be like?"

"Interesting question," Paul responded. "The uranium itself isn't very large, but the container that held it would be of good size. How it was structured so as not to leak radiation is probably a scientific secret, but since it has not been found or used, it may still be secure. *Where* it is being held is the important thing. Commercial storage areas are out of the question. Too many inspections. Sometimes they burn down. Sometimes they are selected for destruction when a new project is planned and they are in the way."

"So?" I put in.

"So it would wind up at a privately owned location not selected for any development and as secure as it is possible to be."

"That really tips the scales in the bad guy's favor, doesn't it?"

"Bad guys like it that way. That's why they're called bad guys."

"What do we do about them, Paul?"

"Hell, buddy, you know the answer to that. You shoot them."

"Great," I said before I hung up.

This may be the information era, but getting the information you want isn't all that easy. You have to give something in order to get something back.

I slouched in my big chair. I took out my two .45's, the Combat Commander and the standard 1911 model. I cleaned and oiled them again, checked the action in each and shoved in full clips. I was a New Yorker even though I didn't like the place, and being in the quietude of Florida's playground didn't exercise my mental facilities at all. I wondered how the hell the other guys could stand it. Maybe I was just too damn mean for retirement.

Telling Bettie that I had to go back to the Big Apple again so soon wasn't easy, but she smiled like she knew this was coming and didn't argue. The way she squeezed my hand told me that she knew this had to be and that she was going to be right here waiting for me to come back wearing a CASE CLOSED smile.

The next morning when I kissed her so long, all I could think of was that she sure would make a great wife for a cop. Even a retired one. And would we be the first retirees in Sunset Lodge to consider starting a family?

The dog gave a puzzled look and whined, but when I petted his head he banged the floor with his tail again.

Chapter Seven

Davy Ross met me at the airport in an unmarked squad car. When I sat back against the seat and buckled up the safety belt, I had that "old times" feeling again.

Davy said, "I know you're not carrying, so I brought you a Glock to wear. They're getting to be standard weapons these days."

I popped open the dashboard compartment and took out the automatic. It was a good gun, but I missed my .45. I opened my belt a notch and bedded it down against my stomach and felt like I was on patrol again.

I told him thanks and he asked me where I wanted to go. He didn't seem at all surprised when I told him to go by our old street again. "Most of it's gone, pal."

"So I'll see the rest. Any vandalism so far?"

"Just some kids breaking windows. Hell, they're going to be smashed up anyway. A couple of vagrants flopped in one house. They have about two weeks occupancy before the wrecking crews get to that building."

"Why so slow?"

"Politics, Jack. Contractors fighting the city, some former occupants still putting up roadblocks, trying to get more money from the local government."

"Think they will?"

"They're still trying," he said. "You know that place where Bucky Mohler lived?"

"Sure."

"Know who built it?"

Davy loved stupid little surprises. "Tell me," I said.

He turned his head. "Big Zappo Padrone, that's who."

Talk about ancient history. "The booze king of Manhattan?"

"The same. Ran a dozen whorehouses, and twenty-three speakeasies in operation, and even before the big crime families got started was the bank for the hoods. Big hoods, that is. Early mob stuff."

"Where do you get all this information, pardner?"

"I read a lot."

"Cops read?"

"Sure. When they're not shooting bad guys."

We turned in the old street at the open end. The station house was gone except for the old brick foundation. Looking toward the other end was like staring in an old fighter's mouth full of broken teeth and a few good ones. Charlie Wing's place was gone, but old Bessie O'Brian's house was still up, and down a ways the restored tenement Bucky Mohler had lived in was intact. Not even the panes were broken in the windows.

"Who's keeping it up, Davy?"

"One of those old city laws. The place was deeded to some big charitable organization. Padrone had a thing about helping down-and-outers."

"Anybody in there now?"

"Hell, even the bums won't go near the place. It's supposed to have some sort of a curse on it."

"Great," I said. "I heard fancy apartments were going in."

"Yeah. And guess who's behind it?"

Another stupid little surprise, I supposed. "Tell me."

"A Saudi investment group."

"Only seems fair."

"Yeah?"

"They took down two buildings, didn't they? Ought to put up a few."

Davy just looked at me.

Right behind us a city Yellow Cab pulled up in front of old Bessie O'Brian's building and a middle-aged woman and old Bessie got out. Davy and I both yelled a big hello and Bessie waved back with a happy yell. "Damn me if it ain't old Shooter! What you doing here, Captain Jack?"

"Saying so long to a friendly old street, Bessie."

"Not so friendly any more."

I walked over, said hello to her daughter from Elizabeth and asked Bessie how she liked the New Jersey countryside.

"Country," she practically screeched. "It's as bad as the Bronx! It's crowded, that's what. No different from the city here."

"You like it?" I asked.

She gave a sly look toward her daughter and whispered, "It's free. My kid's a good cook, too."

I glanced up at the old building she had inhabited for a couple eternities. "What are you back for, Bessie?"

She frowned and tapped her mouth with a wrinkled forefinger. "Left my damn lower teeth behind a slot in the wall back of my bed. Can't eat right without 'em.

Not going to let any more dentists play with my mouth anymore, either. Damn teeth."

"Come on, Bessie, you look great."

"Don't lie to me, sonny. I'm an old hag, I am. You know, I even knew Big Zappo Padrone, you know that?"

I said, "Nope."

"That's his house over there. I was just a kid then."

I nodded.

"Saw that little punk, what's his name...Bucky Mohler over there not long ago. He didn't go in. He was just looking, then he walked away."

"Bessie," I said to her, "Bucky Mohler's been dead a long time. He was killed up in the Bronx years ago."

"The hell he was," old Bessie insisted. "I ain't got teeth, but I sure got eyes, and that was Bucky over there. He was older, but his damn swagger was still there. You remember the way he walked?"

"I remember it all right. Cocky little punk. He didn't do it when I arrested him."

"So arrest him again. He's around somewhere."

"He got buried in a city plot, what was left of him," I told her.

"Baloney," she told me.

"Okay, then. What was he looking at?"

She gave a big shrug, hunching her shoulders. "Beats me. He always was a nosey pig."

"Bessie, Bucky Mohler is dead and buried."

"He's up to something," she said as if she didn't hear me. "Go look. Maybe you'll see what he was after."

It was the only way I was going to get away from the

old biddy, so I gave her a wave and walked down the street and across the pavement to the front of Bucky Mohler's old house. I looked back and Bessie wasn't even watching me.

As the guy used to say on radio, *"So it shouldn't be a total loss, I'll take a look."*

There was a sign on the porch to the demolition crews. The place was not to be disturbed until further orders. Clear enough. They had stayed away. But somebody had been looking. The imprint of shoes on the dusty sidewalk onto the ravaged ground led from one side, stayed close to the house, went completely around it, then turned back almost in the same tracks and stopped by the side door. There was little shuffling around in the dirt. Whoever made those tracks knew exactly what he was doing.

When I checked the dirt residue around the door, scraping it out with a pocketknife, one thing seemed to make sense. That door had been opened recently. There were no indications of forced entry, so someone had a key. It was good lock with a reliable name, a new model, probably installed by the last inhabitants and they wouldn't be hard to check on.

Something was screwy and I didn't like screwy things. Bessie's life was the Street. She knew everything that was going on. If she said she saw Bucky, I'd damn well better check it out.

The city kept pretty good records and it didn't take long for the attendant to locate the book that recorded the death of Bucky Mohler and she gave me the number of his burial plot and its location. But Bucky, or whoever was buried in that plot, would be nothing identifiable by now.

Somehow I couldn't quite discount old Bessie's certainty about seeing Bucky. He'd aged, she'd said, but had still been recognizable—to her, anyway. And if it was Bucky, what was he doing down here on that dead street? A guy like that wouldn't show any nostalgia for a place like this. At least he'd never expect anyone to identify him. The block was almost gone now, the buildings demolished, the few left about to come down. He must have figured there'd be nobody left who could tag him.

Cell phones are great for an area like this. The compartmentalized city of New York had a place for everything and everything was in its place. There was a cubicle where a cop kept track of every known street gang in the city, had IDs on their members, knew their codes and recognition signs and every record of arrests and convictions any of those punks had.

I called the department number and a voice said, "Officer Muncie here. How can I help you?"

"Captain Jack Stang, retired, from the old—"

"Hey, Captain! Good to speak to you. We were talking about you the other day. Somebody saw you down at your old precinct..."

"It's torn down now."

"The new place is pretty nice, I hear."

"Maybe, but not my bailiwick. I got to learn to be a civilian again, you know?"

"Yeah, I guess so. What can I do for you?"

"There was an old Bronx gang, the Blue Uptowners. What happened to them?"

"Hell, Jack, they're still active. A few of the originals are still around, but they're out of the loop. The new kids aren't too bad. Very little trouble."

"Who can I see about something that happened twenty-some years ago?"

"Just a second." I heard him pull some folders out and rustle the papers in them. He wasn't a computer guy either. When he was satisfied, he said, "There's one guy, Paddy The Bull, they called him. His real name was Patrick Mahoney…"

"I recall him," I said.

"He's square now. Has a painting business. Want his address and phone number?"

I said yes, wrote them down in my note pad and thanked Officer Muncie for his time.

Patrick Mahoney was a far cry from Paddy The Bull. He was respectable now, a burly, bald, hard-working guy who had his own business, owned a pickup truck and had a wife and two kids and a big smile when he saw me.

"Damn," he said with a laugh, outside the house in Queens he and a crew were painting, "did I do something wrong?"

"Nope," I said. "You did something right. You grew up."

"It's been a long time, Captain Jack. I coulda been

wearing an orange jailhouse jumpsuit, not these painter's whites, wasn't for you. Now, I know that you're retired and that this isn't a social call, so what's happening?"

"Remember Bucky Mohler?"

He made a face and spit out a dirty word. "He was a lowlife scumbag. Bad news. I tried to tell Wally Chips who ran our club to stay away from him but he wouldn't listen to me. Or a couple of the other guys, either."

"So?"

He paused. His eyes locked onto me, hard. "Look, Captain. You did me a favor once."

"Yeah?"

"You probably don't even remember. You coulda hauled my ass in and I'da done a stretch, a real one—I was over eighteen. You gave me a one-time pass."

I had no memory of it, but if he thought he owed me, fine. "Know something, Paddy?"

He swallowed, then jumped in. "We had a bad apple in our bunch. A squealer. Turned the cops on to us four different times. The guys wanted to bump him, but that would only pull more law down on us, so the rough guys in the club figured out a cute dodge. Bucky, he wanted out from his family and he suddenly had a load of dough to lay out, so if the Uptowners could fake a kill on him and get somebody else in his place, and like really mutilate him up bad, Bucky would put his ID on the body and two birds would be killed with one beer bottle."

"How did Bucky know about your squealer?"

"Man, word gets around, you should remember that."

I bobbed my head in agreement. "What happened?"

"This a clean game you're playing, Captain?"

I squinted at him.

"That was a long way back," he said. "But there's no time limit on murder, is there?"

"No."

"I wasn't in on this play. I came in right after the hit and got details from another member. I don't remember who, either." Something tightened his face. "Captain, there's such a thing as accomplice after the fact, and—"

"Consider this a civilian inquiry."

"You swear it?"

"I swear it."

"Okay," he said and took a deep breath. "I don't know who drove the car, but the deal was when Bucky came up the street the Uptowners would send a member out to identify him and bring him back to us. Our guy would walk on Bucky's left so when the car made the move, Bucky would jump clear and the squealer would get mashed. Well, it worked. The driver went over the body four times and when he finished you couldn't even tell it was human. Bucky took the guy's ID, put his own in its place dropped his jacket or something down and took off."

"No accident investigation?"

"Come on, Captain. Who cared a hoot about a street gang in those days? Just one more punk out of the way. Remember?"

"I remember, but you guys asked for that attitude."

His eyes were steady, unblinking. "And that's why and when I got out of that life, Captain."

"What happened to Bucky?"

"Who knows? He was a downtowner anyway."

Suddenly Paddy The Bull's eyes squinted at me and I asked, "What?"

The old Blue Uptowner said very seriously, "Has he surfaced somewhere?"

"Why, he owe you money?"

"Oh, he paid his tab. He laid a grand on the club with an extra bill thrown in for five hundred. It was a crazy bill, the money itself I mean."

"Crazy how?"

"Crazy weird, crazy odd. Looked real for sure, but was a lot bigger in size than a regular note. It was pinned to the wall in the club until some old guy offered us six hundred bucks for it and everybody had a great beer party."

I grunted. "The government stopped printing those large bills back in the twenties, Patrick me boy."

"No kidding!" Then he asked, "I wonder where he got it from."

I said, "Beats me," but a germ of an idea was infecting my brain. I told him so long and went down to the corner to flag down a cab.

When one came along I sat back and dropped another piece into the puzzle. Old Bessie was right. Bucky Mohler *was* alive. He had something going for him now that could make him the biggest frog in the pond.

And it all had started on the Street that was dying.

*

It's nice being a retired cop.

It's great to have a finely honed reputation too, so that when the desk boys see you go past they think, "*He was a tough apple, that one.*" They're glad to let you in on their knowhow because even if it was a little off the base line, they were doing their duty to protect the citizenry like the men in blue did on the hard pavements.

Nothing much that was exciting ever happened in the development office. They okayed repairs and new building, the papers and inquiries handled between bored clerks. Then an old hotshot comes in, gets instant access to the head man's office and the buzz starts going around.

John Peter Boyle, a grizzled character in an executive's suit, shook hands with a toothy smile and waved me to a chair. "My phone started to ring the minute you came in, Captain."

"Just call me Jack. I'm in civvies now."

He gave me a grin that said he hadn't always been behind a desk. "Come on, Captain—my pop was in World War Two, but afterward he couldn't call Eisenhower 'Ike' to his face now, could he? So...Captain—what can I do for you?"

"Mr. Boyle, I need a permit to inspect a house that's up for demolition."

"Should I ask why?" When I shrugged, he said, "Is this personal?"

"I'm asking as a retired cop."

He shrugged and his grin widened. "In that case, you got it. Want to give me the details?"

*

Before I got back to the Street, I made a short stop at my favorite locksmith's shop on Third Avenue. It had been five years since we'd had any contact, but I didn't have to spell out any details. The round-faced little old guy looked at my face after we shook hands and knew that this wasn't a personal visit.

He said, "Okay, Jack, what's going down this time? Terrorists? Murderers?"

I let him see my grin and said, "I need a key for a Waylord lock. Outside door, oval-shaped key latch, solid brass."

"That's a good standard unit. Nothing special. They used a lot of them on the old tenement buildings a long time ago. You any good at picking that thing?"

"Haven't got the time. Besides, I'm out of practice."

"No sweat, old friend."

He went back to his tiny workshop, came back with two new keys and laid them in my palm.

I said, "How much?"

"Jack, I have another hundred of them. The jokers in those old tenements were always losing theirs, and a new key was cheaper than kicking a door down."

I put the keys in my pocket and winked my thanks at him.

And now I was strictly legal, a permit to secure my entry, a working key to get inside without damaging the property, and a retired cop's ID in my wallet. Absently, I patted my side where the holstered .45 used to hang. Nothing was there.

But the Glock was in my waistband.

*

Shadows were angling down the street now, big, long ones because nothing was there to break them up. Bessie's building was there and her upstairs window was still open, but her elbow pillow was gone. A small corner of a curtain fluttered out, then blew back in again. It was the same curtain that had always been there.

I walked slowly, taking my time, then turned onto Bucky Mohler's concrete walkway and into the shadow of the old structure. In those old days, when Big Zappo Padrone had built the place, it must have been a lulu. There were scars on the building that said a huge porch had once been there and for a grand space around the building there was openness. Hell, this one domicile could have been the only building on the block.

And, like the Street, it was dead.

Or was it?

I merged right in with the shadows and put the key in the lock. It opened easily. I turned the knob and pushed the door open. Nothing was in the way. My miniature flashlight was enough to lead me through the three floors of the building and illuminate dirt and dust that had collected on old-fashioned furniture and rotted rugs on the floor. It was hard to tell if this place had been empty for ten years or a hundred. Nobody had been here in the last five years of my time at the station house. Once, back there in the wild days of city crime, this must have been one hell of a command post. But no sign of that was left any longer.

Without disturbing anything, I went back down the dust-heavy stairs and stopped halfway down. Bucky Mohler had been here. Where were his footprints? Curious.

At the bottom landing another flight of stairs led into the cellar. These weren't fancy like the ones above. They were constructed of heavy planking, wider than usual, bulked up with massive timbering. They didn't even squeak when I went down them. A pair of rats scurried across my path, running from the thin light of my flash. Then I moved the beam across the area.

Except for where I was standing, the entire house was resting on solid earth. There was a coal furnace and electrical boxes next to me, some tools propped against the flatly carved dirt walls. The contractors had most likely laid down the foundation blocks that ran around the house, then just built the rest of the structure up from the dirt. Damn. What kind of building codes did they have then?

Another couple of rats skittered away in the floor debris and I aimed the light down on them. Two pairs of red eyes looked back at me for a couple of seconds, then they broke and ran. I saw in the floor mess what might have been footprints, but nothing I could be certain of.

Something was all out of kilter here. I couldn't tell what it was, but there were ways to find out. When I turned and went back to the stairs, I looked at the shovel and old pickax that leaned against the wall. The pickax was pretty old and the shovel hadn't been used much.

Things had taken a strange turn since I'd been here. It wasn't like the old days when all the crazy details could be laid out before a team of experienced pros and the answers would come back in no time. This business of being retired from the department wasn't all that hot. I still had irons in the fire, and one of them was taking me back to Sunset Lodge.

Davy Ross took me to LaGuardia Airport, and when I got off in Florida, Darris Kinder was waiting for me with the throaty roar of his hopped-up Sunset Lodge police vehicle telling me where he was. "Miss Brice informed me when you were getting in."

"Like coming home again."

"Good trip?" It was a subtle question that only a couple of cops would recognize. He knew damn well something was happening and wanted to know if the waters were calm.

"Very good trip, Darris, but it's not the last."

The answer was enough. He understood what I meant.

And Bettie was waiting on her porch, the dome light behind her showing through her lightweight sundress so she almost looked naked. I heard Tacos make that happy growl of his and dashed out of the car and up the steps to grab my beautiful doll in my hands. I squeezed her waist the smallest fraction before she melted against my chest and her mouth was reaching for mine. It was wonderful wetness that I never wanted to end.

Then Tacos whined and pawed at my leg and Darris

came up and laid my small bag down beside me and said, "Glad to have you back with us, Jack."

"Thanks for the ride, pal."

"Any time. Everything okay in New York?"

"Crazy, but it'll get straightened out." I paused for a little bit and added, "How about here?"

"Under control right now, but something's in the air. You know what I mean? That full moon feeling?"

"I sure do, Darris." I watched his face and he caught the tone of my voice. "We'll talk in the morning, okay?"

He got back in his car, waved me an okay and drove off.

I sat in a rocker beside Bettie and put my hand on hers. The dog saw me and his tail did that floor-banging bit again. I said, "Honey," but got no further.

Bettie said, "I like that word."

So I said it again. "Honey…do you have any…souvenirs from when you worked at Credentials?"

"I'm not sure. Dr. Brice made sure I had a few personal things like that, thinking they might help me some."

"Did they?"

"Not really. I was blind. I couldn't see them."

"Are they here?"

She took her hand out from under mine and stood up. "I'll get them."

Most of her trinkets were what girls would keep in their desks. I wondered how old Dr. Brice had gotten his hands on them. Several were cards with holiday greetings lavishly splashed across them. Two were office photos and one showed the back of an unidentified man talking to her old boss. His face was turned away from the lens; he was a big guy, but beyond that there was no way to identify him. The next picture showed Burnwald with a smaller, younger man dressed in casual clothes and though it only showed part of his face I could tell it was the same young tech in the Credentials pamphlet with the 20th anniversary photo. The man in the picture looked familiar somehow.

I looked at the picture a long minute and Bettie asked, "What's the matter?"

When I described the photograph, she frowned and said, "They must have come out of the collection Florence had. She owned an old Nikon camera and was always snapping shots of anything."

Maybe old Doc Brice had tracked Florence down and, without tipping Bettie was still among the living, somehow snagged some items that he hoped might help jog Bettie's memory. Now, finally, those odds and ends were doing that very thing. And maybe it was time to bring Florence back into the game.

"Think I could find her?"

Bettie raised her eyebrows at the request and said, "It's been a long time, Jack. But I do…I do remember she lived in her family house taking care of her parents. After all these years I'd assume the parents must have died and she'd own the house now. Is that helpful?"

"Maybe. Where was the house?"

"In Brooklyn. Near the Parade Grounds."

"What street?"

"I think it was…" She flipped through mental files,

then smiled as she remembered. "Beverley Road! I think it was Beverley Road."

"Remember the number?"

"Now you're pushing it."

"Can't blame a guy for trying."

"You know...Dr. Brice told me one of the things he was able to turn up was my old address book. It might be in there..."

She got up again and rummaged through her desk drawer and brought out a small leather-bound pad and handed it to me. I found Florence Teal's name, address and phone number and transcribed them into my own notes.

I wasn't going to go back to New York for this information, so I picked up Bettie's phone and dialed the number.

And it was still active.

I asked, "Florence Teal?" when the lady answered and she said, "It's Florence Randall now. Who is this?"

"My name is Jack Stang, ma'am." It was a big secret to share with Bettie's old friend. But Bettie trusted her, and I would have to. "I'm here with someone you used to work with at Credentials—Bettie Marlow."

"That can't be," she told me abruptly. "Bettie has been dead a very long time."

"Presumed dead, Mrs. Randall. How would you like to speak to her?"

"First, who are you?" Her tone was very sharp, though an element of hope was in there, too.

"I am a retired New York City police officer, ma'am.

If you want I can give you my badge number and you can call the city police and verify my identity."

The whole episode must have been a little too heavy for her and she said in an odd tone, "Put Bettie on."

I handed the phone to Bettie.

She said, "Florence, this is me, Bettie. It really is me."

And that was all she had to say.

Her friend recognized her voice at once and I could hear her squeal and watched Bettie laugh with pleasure and for five full minutes they exchanged innocuous information…and one not so innocuous exchange, Bettie making her old friend swear to keep this contact absolutely confidential.

Bettie laid the facts out and I could hear the sharp intake of breath Florence made after each revelation.

Finally, Bettie got to the photos and waited while her friend got out her old scrapbook of duplicates and turned pages until she found the ones Bettie described. The big man's name she didn't know, but he had come in several times over two months to check information in his files.

The other was the young computer repair tech from downstairs. Apparently he must have been working on some difficulty on their floor the day the photo was taken. She remembered he had a "cowboy name."

I wrote that down too.

Bettie stayed on the phone another half hour while I rubbed Tacos' head. The dog would look up at me and bang his tail down on the floor and finally he sat up and put his chin on my leg. I was getting to be a real part of this family.

Bettie asked me, “What’s a ‘cowboy’ name?”

“Like an old-time western star. Tom Mix, Roy Rogers…”

“Who?”

“Before your time, doll.” Before *both* her times. “Listen, do you remember that young computer tech at all? I know I asked you before, but has anything solidified in your mind?”

She shook her head and came back and sat down beside me. “Is it that critical?”

“Non-entities disturb me. His work would have taken him all over the place. He should have been noticed. Remembered.”

“That was a long time ago, Jack. I only seem to recall things when you thrust them right in my face.”

Funny thing for a blind gal to say. “Like what, doll?”

She smiled. “Like calling me ‘doll.’ ”

I ran my fingers through her hair and she nestled against me the way teenagers do and that feeling came back that made me think that a young kid’s body had suddenly been transmitted to an old man’s frame.

“What are you thinking, Jack?”

“Sure you want to know?”

But she already did. She wasn’t all that blind.

My cell phone let out its low signal, killing the moment, and I pulled it out and thumbed the TALK button.

“Stang here,” I said quietly.

"Paul Burke, Jack."

"Hi, Paul. What's up?"

"Some follow-up on that stolen atomic shipment. You all clear down there?"

"Roger. Go ahead."

"Right after the theft, the Feds got a pair of the conspirators and squeezed out some information. It was pretty complicated, so I won't go into it now. But they arranged for the switch right under the noses of the inspecting group and got the container into a waiting truck, drove it to a transfer point where Benny Orbach was waiting to get it to the final point."

I asked, "Paul…you mean that's all the security they had?"

"It was a new twist, Jack. The time before when there was an attempted hijack, eight people got shot, a large transfer truck burned and the cargo was nearly lost. They went the other way this time. Less is more."

"Less is less, Paul."

"Yeah, well. Anyway, it was supposed to be secret."

"*Supposed?*"

"Big money can buy big secrets, Jack. This old world is coming apart. 9-11 should have told us that. So should the mess in Iraq."

"What the heck could anybody use it for? Who else had a delivery system anyway?"

"Jack," he said, "some countries make no bones about atomic materials and use them as a bargaining point. Others are openly trying to develop nuclear weapons."

"Paul, they couldn't have gotten that stuff out of the country, could they?"

"No, not with our inspection devices. But..."

"Say it."

"Suppose they want to use it right here?"

I wanted to explode but held it back.

"What kind of a team is on the prowl for it?" I asked him.

Paul told me, "From what I understand, the Feds have a small army of experts with their noses to the ground."

"All chasing down Benny Orbach's background and current associations?"

"Probably."

"And getting nowhere?"

"I can't find out anything. The big squeeze is on this."

"Have newspapers or TV sources got a bite on the story?"

"No way. The Feds have got long arms with big sticks." He paused for a moment and took a deep breath. "You remember those TV shots of the public running like hell when the World Trade buildings came tumbling down?"

"It hasn't slipped my mind."

"Imagine what would happen if someone popped off one giant atomic blast in the middle of Manhattan."

"Damn!"

"Maybe there wouldn't be anybody left to run away," Paul said hoarsely.

"So we find the load of bad news."

"Who's 'we,' Jack?"

"Guess it's up to the NYPD."

"Jack—stay retired. . . ."

"Oh absolutely," I said derisively.

Chapter Eight

Darris Kinder drove me to a friend of his who operated a towing service and had several pieces of equipment on hand that could handle five tons with no difficulty. Tony Marks, the owner said, "How much weight you talking about?"

"At the minimum, a couple of tons."

"What size?"

"Let's say a four-foot cube."

"No problem. Is it on the ground?"

"In a truck."

"So you slide the skids under it and lift it out." He thought about it, figuring out the next step. "Then," he said, "you spin the load around on the same skids and drop it into the other truck."

"Just like that?"

"Just like that," he repeated. "What are you figuring to steal, Mr. Stang?"

"A lady's heart," I laughed.

"Brother, that *is* a heavy load," he laughed back.

On the way back to Sunset Lodge, Darris said, "Jack, I'm not going to get into your business, but if something is going to happen around here, I'd sure like a little warning."

"It's cool, Darris. If this were a trouble spot, I'd sure tell you."

"Big time, right?" he said.

"Big time," I agreed, "and out of the area."

*

There are moments when you have to sit back and think things out. Other moments, time that seemed to drag on listlessly suddenly explodes into such action that you can hardly remember one second from another. Sometimes—like now—it was a bit of both. I went from being a listless retiree who was turned upside down by things of the past into a hairy old bull with a feather up his tail.

And unlike the immobilized past, the screaming present was unwinding like a high-speed spool of tape on an old-fashioned computer.

So I sat down in my own living room and let the facts roll by me. There weren't many. What could Bettie have uncovered that would lay organized crime open for conviction? It was another generation of mob power now. Did they face the same dangers? What was the stolen atomic pile to be used for? Where was it hidden? It would have to be in a very protected place that could contain possible radiation.

Hell, all I had to do was read the papers. Who wanted atomic energy? Not the kind that could run productive factories or be used in scientific experiments or be beneficial to the citizens of the world.

Somebody wanted the destruction it could bring to cultures they hated. Progress was the 9-11 debacle, the terroristic political regime of Iran and neighboring nations of the same bent. Nothing was hidden any more. All their vicious desires were out in the open now, horrific endeavors barely disguised behind religious themes. With one blast of atomic power there wouldn't be any need for suicide bombings or driving hijacked aircraft into huge commercial buildings. One big city, one gigantic explosion, one tremendous death quotient and their demonic point would be made.

The government had agencies to handle a crisis like this. But the government had agencies that moved as fast as a garbage scow with anchors down. And the government would never think that an almost dead street in Manhattan might be the breeding ground for a great catastrophe.

I ran my fingers through my hair and wondered where all the wild ideas came from. Ideas weren't real—but they preceded reality.

I heard the bells from the ice cream truck coming down Kenneth Avenue. I left bleak thoughts behind and went outside and bought three vanilla super-cones from a kid with a ring in his nose and brought them over to Bettie's house.

Tacos let out those race-dog yips and when Bettie opened the door he nearly took his own personal cone out of my hand, along with my fingers.

Bettie just stood there smiling in her see-through nightie, her untrimmed delta a refreshing pleasure in these days of bizarre pubic buzz cuts.

"Why do I like you?" she asked.

"Because I bring you expensive presents. Like ice cream cones."

The dog had already dropped his on the floor and was busy licking up the mess. I got a paper towel and wiped out the tongue marks from the flooring.

Bettie said to me, "That's the first time they came down this street."

"You said they got fresh, before...?"

"Those drivers were always making remarks to me from the village area."

"You're worth whistling at any place, kid."

"They aren't from around here, you know."

"Now how would you know that?"

"From being blind," she said quietly. "My ears hear things...like dialects, that other people might not recognize. All those drivers have New York accents."

"Most of the people down here are escapees from the big city."

"Sure," she agreed. "But those people have money." She paused. "Do ice cream truck drivers get paid much?"

I shrugged. It was an oddball question. I asked her why.

She told me, "Darris said he thought he saw one of them in Sarasota driving a new Porsche convertible. He had a real snazzy blonde with him, too."

I frowned at that. Porsches don't come cheap, and neither do snazzy blondes.

Of course, Darris could have made a mistake. Except old ex-cops don't make those kinds of mistakes.

I picked up the phone, got Darris on the other end and asked Darris about the ice cream dealer in the Porsche.

There didn't seem to be any doubt in his mind. "I was positive it was him, all right. Maybe I wouldn't swear to it in court, but it sure looked like him."

"You meet him often?"

"When they were getting permission to operate here,

I had a half-hour discussion with him. He checked out at his last job up north. Want me to get out his file?"

"Sure do."

I heard a metal door slide open, the rustling of papers and Darris said, "Here's the skinny on the group that sells the ice-cream product over here."

He read off five names, giving me their backgrounds and I stopped him in mid-sentence with, "Who was that last one, Darris?"

He checked back and said, "Romero Suede. Suede—like the shoes."

"Late twenties, six feet tall, dark, pockmarked complexion?"

"Sounds like the very beauty," Darris replied. "You know him?"

"If it's the same Suede, my old partner nailed him twice for possession of narcotics. He got six months on Riker's Island, did four and was turned loose."

"Who got him off?"

"That came at the request of the city. The place was overcrowded and they needed the space."

"You sure?"

"I'll check it out. Incidentally, where's home base for that ice cream business?"

"That's one of the Garrison projects."

"You know anything about that operation?"

"No," he told me, "But if you want to take a ride to the county seat with me, we can check out the tax rolls and see if we recognize any names."

"You're on, Darris. Pick me up in the morning. You'll give a nice official overtone to the inquiry."

And he did.

Sunset Lodge was a well-respected development and the nature of our requests was simply to see who we might contact to share mutual interests in expansion possibilities.

We got what we needed.

Al Capone liked Florida. So did a lot of other hoods in the old Prohibition days. Some of them drifted down the Keys for retirement, away from the probing of big city cops, or to establish a new line of illegal traffic. For a while Cuba made a great base, then South America opened up a new narcotics trade potential. The ones who got rich went back to being part of the financial underworld, turning dirty money into clean cash.

Retired mobsters weren't just living at Garrison Estates—*they owned it!*

On the way back, Darris behind the wheel of his hopped-up black Ford, I said, "Buddy, I think we're up to our ears in one big, deadly scam."

"*What?*" His voice was soft, but the way he said it was like thunder cracking.

"Do me a favor," I said, "keep a close watch on Bettie. And I mean close. Get one of the station house bunch, or several, to keep a relay cover on her. They know the routine and they know me."

"How about Joe Pender—he was a pal of yours, right?"

"Perfect. And anybody Joe recommends."

"Weapons?"

"Damn right."

"But…"

"The old warhorses'll be glad for the action."

"Jack…these guys are all married."

"I know. You think their wives protested when they were on a hot case?"

He didn't answer me.

I said, "They're cops' wives, pal. They're with us."

"I should have known better than arguing with the Shooter," he told me. "Now, where will you be?"

"Unfortunately, back in the Big City."

"Unfortunately for the Big City," he said.

Something had happened to me.

The Big City had become jammed with those "teeming" throngs that had always seemed so natural before. Suddenly they were all strange faces and behind each face was some odd agony that no one else knew about and the afflicted didn't want to divulge. I used to see these aberrations and try to study them, but this time nothing formed into a clear matrix. I tried to ignore them and go about my business.

Sometimes I'd had to shoot one of them. I didn't like it, but if I hadn't, that one would have shot somebody else. Now, there was that feeling again. Something was happening and it wasn't clear yet. It was arising like an animal awakening from hibernation and it was going to be angry and vicious if anything got in its way.

It was an instinctive gesture, but my hand ran over the familiar bulge that said the old, well-oiled Colt .45 was in its hip holster where it was ready in case all the action was suddenly shoved in my face.

Going into this alone was bad news, so I called

Davy Ross and got him just as he was leaving his office at his new assignment.

I said, "I'm back again, Dave. This thing keeps getting bigger and bigger."

"They all do, Jack. What's going on?"

"I need backup, buddy—this is going to need more hands."

"Want me to alert some of the group here?"

"Tell them to keep their cell phones handy. And their sidearms."

"Got it...and by the way...I got a call to be passed on to you. Remember that vet, Brice, from Staten Island?"

I felt a coldness come down on me like a sudden shower.

"Yeah. What happened?"

"Somebody tried to knock him off. They got into his bedroom and took a shot at him, but one of those pet dogs of his jumped the guy from behind, and the bullet missed. The mutt got his teeth into the guy."

"Bastard get away?"

"Yeah, guy pulled loose, left part of his coat sleeve behind and got into a car that was running outside the office. An old man, a light sleeper, heard the car's engine going and looked out the window to see what was happening and caught the end of the action. Couldn't identify the car and didn't see the plates."

I put the phone down and stared at the wall.

How would they get the connection between Bettie and the vet?

And why? That part was easy...she could have hidden the information that was so critical to the mob there and a hit man was sent to search the place, knocking off anyone who tried to interfere.

There was only one answer. I called Bettie and after four rings she answered.

I said, "Bettie, this is Jack. Did you call Dr. Brice recently?"

"Why…yes. The other day. With my memory returning, I just…just had to. Why? Was that bad?"

"No, kid. Just tell me what happened."

"It was just to say hello and we didn't talk for more than five minutes. He had a sick animal he was tending to." She stopped, then asked quizzically, "Why?"

"You call Darris over now. Like right away. Tell him I said to clean your phone circuitry."

"But…"

"Please, doll, do it. Now."

"Very well." After a brief pause she said, "Is everything all right?"

"It will be," I told her and hung up.

Technology.

It had changed most of the criminal minds so that they knew how to use the greatest scientific advances for their own ends. They had the money to do it and the manpower to make it work. How they knew to tap Bettie's phone was a mystery right now, but all mysteries finally get solved sooner or later.

There was another part of the puzzle that was evident now. If they knew where she was, why didn't they kill her?

Because she still had something vital they needed, and that was buried in her lost memory.

Then something else flittered through my mind. How did the mob *know* she had lost her memory? Nothing was ever printed in the papers except the fact that she had been presumed killed when the car went over the bridge.

There was a damn leak.

Someplace in her past, someone knew of the infirmity and somehow passed word to somebody else and the news went unheeded until someone recognized it for what it was. It couldn't have been a reporter because that was a story that would never be suppressed. The whole affair was damned accidental and had taken a long time before it raised its head from the dust.

For a few minutes I thought about it and the conclusion had to be one thing. An employee at the veterinary hospital had overheard something, or was told something in confidence, and had unknowingly passed the information to someone who realized the implication and went to the right people with the story.

But… The big *but* was still there. Where did she hide the essential piece of information that had disrupted so many lives? And what was it?

You can hate coincidences all you want, but they happen.

There was one oddball piece of information nobody had bothered to investigate. Big Zappo Padrone's name had come up, like a wild throw from left field. He'd been dead for generations, a lousy racketeer from the days when they were throwing bombs into saloons selling the wrong guy's beer and blasting away with sawed-off shotguns and outrunning the Coast Guard boats with those hot rod, Liberty-powered engines left over from World War One.

He'd lived on the same street I'd worked on. His old house had been the headquarters for the New York mob action. Smaller then, not nearly as efficient as now, but just as deadly.

I glanced at my watch, then grabbed a cab and took it to the big library on Forty-second Street. I didn't even have to show my credentials. The librarian recognized me, gave me a big welcoming smile and directed me to the area where all the old newspapers had been filmed and were on file for immediate usage.

It didn't take long to zero in on Big Zappo's background. There were old photos of his house on a nearly empty street, and one close-up with Big Zappo himself on the porch trying to hide his face behind a newspaper. I was just about to turn the dial on the microfilm reader and see the next page, when my eye caught something that damn near made me sweat.

The house number was plain as day. It was 4428. Hell! I remember Bucky painting on 703 when I was at the station house at the corner!

This old street ran crosstown and in the wild, hairy days of Big Zappo, one end of the street was growing and the other end just dropped into the East River. When the building boom started to corral the immigrants, streets got numbered and houses were re-identified. 4428 turned into 703. So, who hung onto the old number and why? There was a connection, all right. It was Big Zappo himself. He had lived there under *both* addresses.

But Big Zappo was dead. He had been dead a long time.

Then what was so blasted important about that house?

Bucky Mohler.

He'd lived in that house but took nothing from it. He'd helped kill another kid so he could disappear. Why? Where had he gone into hiding? There was one place...a decent job. Nobody would ever suspect Bucky Mohler of being able to get and keep any kind of respectable employment.

I let out a little grin and said silently to myself, okay, Captain of the station house, big cop with medals, well trained to recognize clues and twists of circumstance, how did you miss this one? You saw the picture, wrinkled your nose at the partial face shot because you thought he looked familiar to you and didn't push it any further.

You saw pieces of him in *two* pictures, didn't you? That Credentials anniversary pamphlet and the office photo.

No wonder you're retired.

Bucky Mohler was the young guy, the computer whiz, the fix-it guy at Credentials, the one in the office photo Bettie had shown me!

Chapter Nine

The street was a rubble-strewn war zone now. The utilities were off and the vagrants chased out and on the stretch down from where the station house used to be, only two buildings remained.

Old Bessie's former domain was five vacant lots away from the tenement that had once belonged to a gangster named Padrone.

John Peter Boyle at the development office took my questions over the phone and called back with the answers. He confirmed that a charitable organization operating homeless shelters owned the building. This had held things up, but the charity rep said a deal had been worked out with both the city and the new Saudi ownership. In two days, the building known in its time by two numbers—703 and 4428—would be just another pile of debris.

"But here's the funny thing," Boyle said. "Funny odd, I mean—the kind of circumstance that doesn't get into the public record."

"Not following you."

"It's just this, Captain—the rep of that charitable group mentioned that they had a sort of silent partner in that old building. Dating back to when the ownership was transferred over to them."

"Interesting."

"The old tenement was renovated twenty years ago,

you know—nothing fancy, just efficiency apartments. Still, it generated decent revenue."

"Housing in the big city always does."

"Yeah, until lately. You know what that neighborhood's been like, last five or six years. That building either needed another renovation or a wrecking ball."

"And the latter is what it'll get."

"Cheaper for these developers to put up new buildings than try to gentrify these old tenements, even one that had been renovated a couple decades ago."

"Understood," I said. "You get the silent partner's name?"

"Yeah, and you'll love it: John Smith. Lives upstate somewhere. Address is a P.O. Box. Look, Captain, I didn't dig deep—this was a friendly conversation, off the cuff…and I could tell if it got serious, the charity rep might clam up."

"It can be tracked…."

"You're the detective."

"Mr. Boyle, you're not a bad one yourself."

Two days, and 4428 would be rubble and dust.

Two days for something to happen, if that old pile of brick and wood and glass really meant a damn thing.

But two days was also manageable. I could set up an operation within those parameters, no problem.

Which is how I ended sitting at old Bessie's window. I didn't hang out over the sill—she had taken her red velvet elbow pillow with her, and anyway I didn't want to be seen. This was surveillance.

And like all surveillance duty, it had its drawbacks. The stripped shell of the tiny old apartment, with its faded floral wallpaper and ancient creaky floors, stunk with decades of cooking smells. I never saw a rat, but I could hear them in the walls and halls, tiny claws scratching, scurrying.

But I was looking for a bigger rat, name of Bucky Mohler.

Mohler had been a gang kid coming up strong, back in the old days, an up and comer who suddenly up and went. The old gal who'd sat in this very window had seen his return, and I hadn't believed her at first.

I believed her now.

With no heat in the building, and the fall air turning from crisp to cold, I was glad to be in a black corduroy jacket over a black sweater. The .45 was on the hip of my black jeans. I looked half cop, half ninja.

The dark attire was strictly in case Bucky showed up after sundown. But I doubted he would. With the street damn near dead, and only a few street lamps to light the way, Bucky returning in the daylight made sense.

I intended to put in the long day shift myself, seven AM till nine PM. For nightshift duties, I had lined up retired brother cop Pudgy Gillepsie for the first night, and an off-duty Sgt. Davy Ross himself for the second one.

The officials were in the know, but I was playing a hunch. Or call it an educated guess, yet none of the evidence that provided that education would be enough to get the NYPD or the Feds on the front line. A phone call, though, would bring the cavalry on the run....

I didn't mind a long surveillance. I'd done it enough times, and for every splashy shoot-out the papers had written up from my so-called exploits, there were a hundred days of dull damn tedium. If pressed, I'll admit my bones and muscles did some complaining. With sixty looming up ahead like a speed limit sign, I was bound for a little discomfort.

Luckily I'd been able to improvise. A few abandoned items of furniture were to be found in Bessie's building, including a well-worn lounger that a thrift shop would've junked, but it still allowed me to sit looking out that window at the Padrone building like I was watching football or an old movie on the tube.

As the guy who was throwing this party, I had brought along a Styrofoam ice chest filled with Cokes and Millers. Also a grocery bag filled with bags of chips and four plastic-bagged sandwiches—Swiss cheese and pastrami from a good deli. Wanted to do right by my pals helping me out, plus I had to eat, too.

I spoke to Bettie by cell phone in the morning and she reported nothing suspicious. On the other hand, nothing got past her—she was aware that I had Darris Kinder and Joe Pender keeping an eye on her.

"Darris stopped by yesterday morning," she said, "and Joe came by in the evening—just saying hello, seeing if I needed anything. But it's more than that, isn't it, Jack?"

"Yes," I said. "Something's about to happen."

"What?"

"Tell you the truth, I'm not exactly sure. I know the New York end is coming together. That young computer tech at Credentials, twenty years ago—he was a kid named Bucky Mohler."

"I wish I could say that name means something to me."

"That's a stray piece that may float back yet. But it was him, all right—your friend Florence said the computer tech had a 'cowboy' name. Well, when I was a kid, there used to be a cowboy actor called Buck Jones."

"Who?"

"Before your time, kitten. Before your time even twenty years ago…but not Florence's, and that's what she meant, I'm sure. Buck. Bucky."

"Jack…you say twenty years ago, this Bucky worked where I worked, at Credentials, on computers. But what does that have to do with today?"

"I'm not sure. I think the answer is right here in the big city." I looked out the window at the Padrone building, old and not quite proud. "And when I get it, I'll fly home to you."

"Fly fast, Jack."

"Baby, I won't even need a plane."

Phone calls broke the monotony of the stakeout. Some I made, some were incoming, like the one from police scientist Paul Burke.

"Got something on that carved ivory hash pipe, Captain."

"Great! Don't tell me you actually got a print off that thing?"

"I actually got a print off that thing—a partial. But that was enough to make a match through other means.

The print likely belongs to a convicted drug dealer, a sterling citizen name of Romero Suede."

"I've heard of him."

"Oh? He's got a rep as a mean one. Questioned on several murders, but never charged. Served his drug-bust time, no outstanding warrants—but also no current address."

I knew what Romero Suede's current address was: Garrison Properties, Florida.

"How I know this partial is likely Suede's," Burke was saying, "comes from a letter in his file. The warden commending Suede for his 'artistic endeavors'—wood and ivory carving."

"The guy is carving out hash pipes in stir and the warden commends him for it?"

Burke chuckled. "Well, Jack, the prison system *is* trying to get its charges ready for the outside world again.... By the way, there were traces of high-quality hash in that pipe."

"Thanks, Paul."

"Always happy to help a retiree enjoy his sunshine years."

"And you could stick it where the sun *don't* shine, buddy."

He laughed, so did I, and we rang off.

That afternoon, between cold Millers, I spoke to Captain Kinder.

"You got Bettie covered, Darris?"

"Damn straight. Working the dayshift myself, Jack. And Joe is on nights. Plus, we have every ex-cop on your street, and the street behind you, alerted that something may go down and soon. All they do is nod. They don't even ask what."

I grinned at the cell. "Old firehorses just need to hear the bell, Darris. They don't ask where the fire is, just follow the smoke."

"One thing I'm keeping a close eye on, Jack, is our friendly neighborhood ice cream trucks. We've had two trolling Sunset today."

"How much ice cream does a retirement village need, anyway?"

He grunted. "It's not so suspicious that I can collar 'em or anything. We've always got a lot of grand-kiddies visiting down here, and for the Golden Age crowd, there's nostalgia value in buying ice cream goodies off an old-fashioned truck. These guys really do have plenty of customers to justify their presence."

"I think you'll find those trucks are hauling more than ice cream."

"What, drugs? You don't think our fellow ex-coppers are buying their prescription drugs on the black market, do you? Weed for glaucoma patients, maybe?"

He sounded like he wasn't sure if he was kidding or not.

"That's not what I was thinking, Darris. Garrison Properties, right on the ocean there, is a convenient spot to offload narcotics from South America."

"Yeah.... And with a housing development populated by retired mobsters and their families going in, who's going to police that little action?"

"Nobody," I said, "and nobody. Also, our favorite ice-cream salesman, Romero Suede, is probably at least using drugs if not selling."

"That's probably a reasonable assumption, Jack—but how did you make it?"

I told him about Paul Burke tying the hash pipe I'd found at Garrison Properties to Suede.

"I don't suppose that hash content is enough for us to bust his ass," Kinder said.

"No. What with lab work done unofficially for us in New York, and only a partial print. But it confirms we're correct in giving Mr. Suede our full attention."

Kinder grunted his agreement, assured me Bettie was under his watchful eye, and signed off.

Later I checked in with Kinder's helper, Joe Pender.

"Your wife getting on your case, Joe, about you getting back in temporary harness?"

"Hell no," he laughed. "I think she likes having me out from underfoot. Gets the whole damn double bed to stretch out in, plus a pass for a few nights on my snoring.... Listen, can I make a suggestion?"

"Sure."

"After nightfall, why don't we move Bettie out of her place, and into yours? If we manage to do that without anybody unfriendly spotting it, that puts any home invaders invading the wrong home."

"Not a bad idea. And the layout of both houses is pretty much identical, so she won't have too much trouble getting her bearings."

"Jack, you better call her and suggest this. Kinder

and me, we haven't clued her in that we're watching her. That, you know, we think trouble's brewing."

I laughed. "Joe, she's way ahead of all of us. But I'll call her."

Through that morning and afternoon, I went through a single sandwich and two bags of chips and three Millers. The water in the building was off, but the toilet in Bessie's apartment didn't protest when I took the occasional piss. I'd be lying if I said I didn't catch myself starting to doze off a couple of times, and one of those times was at dusk.

And just as my body did that little startled dance after you fall asleep for a second, I came fully awake to see a late-model Buick, light blue, nothing special, pull in at the Padrone tenement.

And by pull in, I mean literally. The driver came up and on over the sidewalk and across the ground and around behind the building, snugging the vehicle back there. When he emerged, the driver was wearing a zippered navy blue jacket and tan pants and running shoes.

Funny thing was, though he was trying to stay careful, surreptitious even, he couldn't get the swagger out of his stride. That same cock-of-the-block walk that old Bessie had recognized.

Bucky Mohler.

Changed but not changed—still a medium-sized, smirky round-faced guy with squinty eyes and brown hair, only thinning now, like lines drawn on a cue ball with a felt-tip pen.

He entered the building the same way I had, the time I'd gone in to poke around. And when that side door closed, I was off my lounger and heading out of the empty apartment to run down those old stairs.

Only I was halfway out the front door of the building, onto its stoop, when I had to duck right back. Then I settled into a position where I could peek around and not be seen even as I saw another vehicle pulling in at the Padrone building.

The van was black and unmarked—shiny and new, and when it backed in as near as possible to Big Zappo's side door, the vehicle shuddered to a stop and somehow conveyed heaviness. The tires were oversize, too.

Was I reading in, or was that van designed to carry a large load for its size?

I felt a spike of excitement shoot up my spine. The kind of tingles I hadn't felt since I'd been officially on the Job were like little needles jabbing my neck....

Four guys got out of the van—two from the front, two from doors opening at the rear. The two from in front wore black leather jackets, not the motorcycle variety, more like something out of a men's fashion magazine. They looked much alike, dark-complected with devil's mustaches and goatees, only one was much taller—a Middle Eastern Mutt and Jeff. Their pants were black, too—also leather? Shoes had a gleam.

The two from in back were brutes—one bald, one with a ponytail, both with well-trimmed full-face beards, also copper-complected. They wore black jumpsuits and heavy work boots. And heavy gloves.

The fashion plates in black leather went in first, the muscle following—management trailed by labor. No sign of Bucky. No way to know if he was expecting this company, or getting ambushed.

Either way, I was interested.

I stayed away from the sidewalk and the yellow pools of lamplight, and ran in back of the buildings that were the last two teeth in the street's horrible smile. Keeping low, like I once did in a far eastern jungle, I felt ridiculous; no ferns or brush to aid me, just open devastation where the life along this street had been.

I was careful slipping into the building. It seemed possible, even probable, that one of the bruisers would be left to guard the door. Since nobody had been posted outside, that meant just inside the door was more likely.

Since I still had a key to the front, I went in that way, quietly, but with the .45 in my fist. The building was already dark. With the electricity off, and the blue of dusk outside darkening every second, the going had to be slow and careful. When I made it down to the side door, however, where a burly sentry might have waited, nobody was on guard.

For a few moments I just stood there, wondering if they'd all slipped out while I was making my careful way here.

Then I heard the voices below.

The voices didn't echo, but they rattled and shook the old rafters and planks and sound seeped up through a thousand nooks and crannies. The voices were not raised, and Bucky seemed to be dealing with expected guests, not a surprise party.

By the time I reached the landing onto those heavy, timber-backed stairs to the basement, I could see that an orange-tinged glow of light came from down there. And I could hear the conversation clearly.

"You have the combination, Mr. Mohler?"

"Yeah. Of course I do. Years ago, see, I hired a safe-cracker pal of mine to open this baby up. Found a lot of loot in there. Old, old loot, big oversized bills from way back when."

"Most interesting."

But the voice, which had a pronounced Middle Eastern accent, didn't sound that interested.

And I was hearing more than conversation—somebody was digging down there. A couple of somebodies, probably the two jump-suited, bearded brutes, making use of the shovel and pickax I'd spotted on my previous trip here, tools that had been leaned against one carved-out dirt wall.

I risked moving down the first step. A good six steps could be mine before anybody spotted me, unless they looked up and in my direction. The stairs remained in the darkness, the central area of the cellar lighted by a couple of electric Coleman lanterns on either side on the dirt floor, like at a campsite.

So I risked another step. Like a damn ballet dancer, I placed my foot just right, and got no squeak or creak in return for my artistry.

By the time I got to the third step, I could hear a broom down there, sweeping away dirt.

If they'd turned around, they could have seen me—me and my .45. But down there in the orange-ish glow of the Coleman lanterns, all of their backs were to me, except Bucky's, and his attention, like theirs, was on the big old iron object that the digging and sweeping had uncovered in the dirt floor.

It was the face of a massive safe, maybe close to a hundred years old, with a combination dial and a big metal latch. The perfect place to hide a huge stash of cash. *And the perfect place to hide, say, a four-foot atomic cube worth millions and packing mass destruction potential....*

The four men meeting with Bucky had to be Saudis tied to the group that had bought and killed this old street, and who were vying to kill a lot more streets, maybe in this very town. The thought flashed through my mind that these bastards might be planning to turn this building itself into a bomb, to assemble their weapon right in this basement in this forgotten stretch of urban landscape in the middle of everything.

Only, they had that specially rigged van out there. And the two muscle men with work boots and gloves on. So they were here to load up the atomic cube and make for points unknown—say, Florida....

Bucky was on his hands and knees in the dirt, leaning over the massive safe, which had so many years ago been buried on its back in the basement of a gangster's lair. He was down in the dirt in more ways than one, selling his soul and his country out to a bunch of slobs who weren't satisfied with all that oil money, no. They had to take out the infidels, too. Hell, weren't we their best customers? Hadn't we paid for those black leather jackets with the matching pants these clowns were modeling?

Of course, we couldn't offer them seventy virgins in heaven or Valhalla or wherever the hell they thought they were headed. Scrounging up seventy virgins in the big city at this stage was a stretch....

After the twisting and clicking of the combination dial, Bucky worked the latch and, standing with one foot on the dirt and another on the lower edge of the iron safe, yanked and the door yawned open with a creak worthy of a haunted house.

And all four of Bucky's houseguests leaned forward, throwing shadows in the Coleman light, agape with anticipation: now they could see down in, behold what the old safe held.

So could I, from my perch on the third step.

Nothing.

The damn thing was empty!

Bucky's head whirled, his eyes wide with shock and fear, and the shorter black-leather Saudi slapped him with a nine millimeter that sent the traitor tumbling down into the open safe.

And Bucky was on his back like a bug.

"What happened to the item we purchased, Mr. Mohler?" This was the other Saudi, the taller one. No emotion on the surface of the bass voice but something constricted it down low. "Where has our purchase gone?"

"I don't know, I tell you! I don't *know!* Somebody

beat me to it—stole the damn thing from under us! You think I'd invite you guys here if—"

The gunshot sounded weird—like the voices, it didn't as much echo as cause a minor tremor in the ancient rafters. Dust and grime drifted down like dirty snow. The big lead box Bucky was down in gave up a kind of metallic mini-echo, but that was mostly drowned out by Bucky screaming.

Getting shot in the knee will make a man do that.

Scream.

The smaller Saudi said calmly, "Who did you tell? You compromised this purchase, at the minimum. Who did you *tell*, Mr. Mohler?"

Well, I couldn't have them killing the punk. Bucky still knew things I didn't. And as much as I wouldn't have minded seeing a guy who would sell out a city getting another kneecap or maybe his gonads shot off, I had to put a stop to this.

I came clattering halfway down the reinforced steps, not trying to be quiet at all, pointed the .45 and yelled, "NYPD! Weapons down, hands up!"

But every one of them got stupid. All at once stupid, if not exactly otherwise coordinated—they turned toward me, looking almost red in the lantern light, and went for their guns and by all rights one of them should have been fast enough.

I took the little leather-jacket one out first—both he and the taller Saudi were on my left, with the burly boys at right, Bucky squirming on his back down between them. By shooting the short one first, exploding his head like a melon with a forehead-centered .45 that splashed the taller one with gore, I distracted tallboy for the fraction of a second I needed to give him the same skull-shattering treatment.

Neither one had fallen by the time I swung the .45 onto the bigger, slower brutes, who were digging in their waistbands for Glocks, their hands clumsy in the work gloves. Still, the one closest to me almost had his rod out.

There wasn't time for anything fancy—I just unloaded the .45 on them, head and torso alike, one bullet squirting the juice out of the bald one's left eye, the ponytail guy losing an ear before catching a hell of a heart shot and they collided with each other doing their stringless puppet routine, tumbling in a bloody pile-up.

The rafters shook and dust and dirt rained down and the blood on the dirt floor draining from shattered skulls and punctured organs was already seeping and soaking in, shiny and glittery, black not red.

Blood mist and cordite were mingling as I took my time coming down the steps, putting a new clip in just in case reinforcements showed.

"Doctor!" Bucky was yelling, having a spasmodic fit down in his iron box.

"I'm not your doctor," I said, "but here's what I prescribe for you, Bucky."

And I clanged the door shut on him.

His muffled screams made me smile.

A minute or so later, I opened the safe and leaned

down in and stuck the .45 in his face. "Selling a nuke to terrorists, Bucky—new low even for you."

"Shooter? Shooter! Don't do it, don't *do* it...."

"I have to, Bucky."

"Don't do it!"

"I said I have to. Much as I want to kill your greedy ass, I'm going to haul you up and out and get you a doctor."

"God bless you, Captain! God bless you...."

"Why, Bucky—did I sneeze? But if you don't talk, and tell me every damn thing I want to know, after I get you to a medic? The only blessing you'll get is a death as quick as these bastards got."

I didn't call 911—I called Sgt. Davy Ross. While Bucky and I were waiting down in that cellar of death for his ambulance and my cop pal, I gave him enough first aid on the shot-up knee to get by. I had him sit on the edge of the open safe. It stank of vacated bowels in that dank space and, in that orange Coleman glow, it was a hellish atmosphere that even got to me a little. But it really got to Bucky.

He passed out and I'd have to wait to ask him my questions. That was okay. Even if he was faking, I didn't figure he was in shape for much of a getaway run.

Chapter Ten

Bucky really rated.

Ross arranged him a private room at Bellevue's prison ward. There, in a bed where his shot-up bandaged leg was elevated, Bucky was feeling no pain, thanks to the medics pumping him full of junk.

Not that Bucky didn't feel the weight of his circumstances. That smirk of his was gone, and I didn't figure after he finally got back on his feet he'd ever have that same swagger old Bessie recognized.

"I'll cooperate," he said. He was cranked up in the bed enough to be able to look right at me and the police sergeant standing at his bedside. "I'll give you the names of those Saudis, every damn one of them creeps."

Ross said, "We don't need their names, Bucky. Captain Stang here shot them all."

"There are *others!* I'm going to want immunity. You want my cooperation, I'm going to want immunity."

I said, "You'll want a lawyer, too."

"That's right!"

I turned to Davy and said, "Why don't you go get him one?"

Davy saw the look in my eyes and smiled just a little. "I'll go and get right on that."

And Sgt. Ross was gone.

"Now it's just you and me, Bucky," I said, hovering

over him. "Not a cop and a con. Just a couple old birds from the street."

"Don't shit me, Shooter! *You're* a cop!"

I braced my hand on the mattress near his pillow. "I retired."

"You said I need a lawyer..."

"You do. For when the cops are around. Before that happens, you and me are going to catch up on old times. The room isn't wired, and nothing you say can be...but you know the rest."

Beads of sweat pearled the forehead under the skimpy cue ball comb-over. "Why should I talk to you, Shooter?"

"Because I saved your ass. And because you promised you would, if I got you a medic. I kept my promise, Buck." I shifted my position and very gently laid my hand on his elevated, bandaged knee. "Your turn to keep yours."

It all came spilling out.

How twenty years ago a mob guy named Benny Orbach buttonholed him about Big Zappo's safe. A big heist was going down, involving atomic materials, and the right kind of storage was needed for the dangerous stuff. That old lead safe of Padrone's would do the trick, till the haul was shifted to a buyer. And there were lots of prospective buyers on the scene, even back then—from the North Vietnamese to various Middle Eastern groups.

"How did you happen to have access to Big Zappo's safe, Bucky?"

"I found it—I heard the stories about Zappo's money

stash being somewhere in that cellar, and I looked till I found it."

"How much loot did you find?"

"Not that much—maybe ten K in those big old bills. If I'd known they was collector's items, I wouldn't have been so free with 'em."

"Why did you have access, Bucky? Why do you have part ownership of that building?"

"Because...because I'm Big Zappo's kid, all right?"

"What?"

"*Bastard* kid, okay, Shooter? He was old enough to be my granddad when one of his whores had me, get it? But blood is blood, and he willed that building to me. He set it up that half of the income went to that charity—my old man had a thing about helping out these homeless characters."

"They say he started those soup kitchens back in the Depression."

Bucky nodded. "And, tell you the truth, Big Zap thought I'd just sell the place and blow the dough, if there wasn't some, you know...constraint put on me. I was a wild-ass kid, in those days—you remember. Hell, my share was tied up in a trust fund deal till I turned forty!"

He was at least fifty now.

I asked, "Why didn't you sell out then?"

"Because I wasn't a snotnose no more. You might not buy it, Shooter, but I've led a respectable damn life, for years. Even twenty years ago, I'd already broke off from that whole street gang scene—I took a technical course. Got in the ground floor of computer repair."

"Which is how you got the Credentials gig."

Again he nodded. "Yeah. And when Benny Orbach came around there, he recognized me. He knew me as this kid who used to be a runner for Big Zappo, and remembered the safe in the cellar."

Orbach must have been the other guy in Bettie's office photo, the big guy with his back to the camera.

"What was Orbach doing at Credentials?"

"This atomic heist, it was already in the works. Orbach knew his ass was on the line, getting involved with something that big—I mean, it's the kind of crime you do federal time on. There are people who consider that kind of heist, you know...unpatriotic or some shit."

"The word is treason, Bucky."

Despite all the junk he was on, Bucky had a hysterical edge in his squeaky voice. "Listen, I didn't even know what was gettin' heisted. I only figured it out later, when it got in the papers. All I knew was, Orbach needed a lead-lined vault for something hot."

Something really hot.

"But you knew Orbach was laying his ass on the line," I reminded him.

"Yeah, but not *why*. Later, I put that together."

I leaned in closer. "The girl, Bucky—the girl Bettie Marlow. Why *her*? Why was she abducted?"

He smiled but it looked sick. "I don't know, Shooter. Honest, man, that was nothing I was part of. But I can guess...."

"Guess then."

"See, it's what you asked before—Orbach, he put

together a big file on everything he knew about the East Coast mobsters. Real insider stuff. Names, dates, you name it."

"Why?"

"Orbach thought with a high-risk caper like this, he should take out an insurance policy. If he got caught, if he took this rap, he wanted to know he'd be safe in stir. That nobody would slip a shiv between his ribs, in the lunch line, to make sure the feds didn't get the real skinny on who was behind the atomic heist."

"And the young woman who worked at Credentials?"

He paused, his eyes jumpy.

Then he blurted, "Why don't you just *say* it, Shooter?"

"Say what, Bucky?"

"That she was your girl! You were going to marry her, right? Don't pretend she isn't what this is all about."

I felt the muscles along my spine twitch.

"You *knew*, Bucky?" I said, keeping my tone steady. "Back then, you knew about Bettie and me?"

This nod was hesitant, then followed by two quicker assertive ones. "And when I saw Orbach at Credentials, and figured out that the *Shooter's* girl had been the one who'd entered the mob data he'd entrusted to them? Well, then I knew Orbach was screwed."

My hand clenched the edge of his pillow. "And you *told* him?"

"No! I swear I didn't."

It was hard work keeping my voice steady, but I managed. "Why not, Bucky? Why didn't you tell Orbach?"

"Because...because I told the guys I was working for instead."

I swallowed hard, but I kept my expression calm. "Mob guys, you mean."

"Yeah. See, I…Shooter, I'm going to level with you. I'm going to level with you because it's my best shot at not really pissing you off. And all I want right now is to not piss you off, okay?"

"Okay."

Now Bucky spoke slowly, as if to a child. "The reason I was working at Credentials was because some top-secret government stuff was going through there. I don't know why some little hole-in-the-wall computer outfit had such confidential federal dope on file, and I don't know how the guys I worked for knew, neither. But they had stuff on file, all right, information about weapons and munitions stolen from federal armories… and about sales of the stuff to foreign countries. Enemy countries."

"Why was that of interest to mobsters?"

"Because this atomic shipment was coming through, and the heist was all planned and everything…and they needed to know the players."

"The potential buyers, you mean."

"What else? That was what I was trying to get for them, that info…and my computer repair job with Credentials, that was my cover."

"And did you get that info, Bucky?"

"Hell, yes. Stealing candy from a baby."

"What about the files on your mob pals that Orbach left with Credentials?"

He shrugged. "I erased the sons of bitches. Wiped the computer drives clean. Used a magnet on the back-up discs, too." His eyes tightened. "Only, I knew your girl..." But the words caught in his throat.

"Spill it, Bucky."

His eyes were wild. "Shooter, now I'm *leveling* with you, man, you need this information, don't go apeshit on me, man."

"You give me what I need, Bucky, you never had a better friend."

"Okay. Okay. This was a long time ago, and I was a stupid greedy little punk who didn't know right from wrong."

I decided not to remind him he'd been trying to sell the guts of a nuke to terrorists earlier this evening.

"Go on, Bucky."

"I...I knew Bettie, knew she'd made copies of the files and took 'em home with her. And I knew she was your girl, and it was obvious that she was going to turn 'em over to you."

If I smothered him with a pillow, no one would hear. If I covered his face with a pillow and used it to muffle the .45, no one would hear that either.

"Don't...don't look at me like that, Shooter."

"They're still after her, aren't they, Bucky?"

"I wouldn't know, honest, man, I wouldn't know! I had no idea they was going to snatch that snatch of yours!"

My hand clenched the pillowcase cloth again.

"Shooter, you got to believe me, I wanted no part of that shit. Why do you think I paid to fake my damn death? I wanted out, I *got* out, disappeared upstate and I been straight ever since. Computer repair, to this day. You think it's easy keeping up on this computer crap, competing with these kids who had computers in their damn playpens?"

"I feel for you, Bucky. But like the man says, I just can't reach you."

"Shooter…Shooter…."

"If you went straight, what were you doing back in the big city, on that street, in that old building?"

"I saw in the papers Orbach was out of stir and then right away he bought the farm. So I kind of started thinking about the safe and what was in it, and how I must be the last one to know about it. And how, you know, valuable them contents was."

"Why would a straight successful businessman start thinking bad things like that, Bucky?"

"I *told* you it's been tough, competing. Plus I lost everything in my divorce, and…but it was just me thinking. I didn't do anything about it. Not at first."

"Oh?"

A short nod. "Then when those Saudi guys contacted me about buying the old building, I checked on the atomic stash and, damn, if it wasn't still there! Orbach dead, and so many of the old mob guys gone. Why not make a buck?"

"So the Saudis didn't approach you about the contents of that safe?"

"No—they're developers. They're going to build friggin' condos or something. But I figured they might be connected to, you know, certain kinds of people. You know—crazy ragheads with money to burn."

My stomach tightened, muscles twitching, but I didn't let it show in my face.

"And so you told them about what you had for sale."

"Yeah! Of course. Wouldn't you?"

I let that pass. "And they were interested?"

"Not for themselves, but they got in touch with people who were. I guess that box of plutonium or whatever the hell it is, it's something people have been looking for, for years."

"Yeah. Only the safe was empty."

His shook his head, eyes wild again. "Shooter, I checked that baby. I opened that safe and there it was, wrapped up in blankets just like when the heisters stuck it in there. Twenty years ago!"

"So you were double-crossed."

"Not by the Saudis. You were there, Shooter. You saw how that went down. Somebody else got to that stash between the last time I checked it and when I opened up the safe for my buyers."

"Who?"

"Hell, I don't know. I didn't advertise this thing. Only a handful of higher-ups in the mob knew about the atomic heist, and of course everybody but Orbach got killed when they kidnapped your Bettie."

I leaned close. "They're still looking for her, Bucky. Why?"

"Not for what was in that safe, Shooter! No way. But they could still be afraid of those files. Those floppy discs."

"Why, after all this time?"

"Some guys Orbach implicated are still alive. That was one hell of an insurance policy, Shooter—names, dates, places. Man, even now, there'd be hell to pay with the coppers and the feds."

I heard something behind me.

Davy Ross was peeking in.

He said to Bucky, "A public defender's on the way, Mr. Mohler."

"Thanks, Sergeant." Bucky looked at me with eyes that were afraid to blink. "Are we cool, Shooter? Did I give you what you need?"

"I need one other thing."

"What, Shooter?"

I leaned in and whispered; this was nothing Davy needed to hear.

"When this is over, assuming you don't wind up in a federal pen somewhere, and you see me coming? I need you to go the other way as fast as your new kneecap will allow."

He swallowed. "I've had better best friends."

"No you haven't. I saved your life six times today."

He squinted at me. "Six?"

"Once in that cellar, and five times in this room when I talked myself out of killing you."

Chapter Eleven

We were sitting at the kitchen table in number 820 on Kenneth Avenue in Sunset Lodge—my one-and-a-half story digs, where Bettie had moved in at Joe Pender's suggestion and with Darris Kinder's approval. Tacos was sleeping on a braided rug nearby, next to his dog dishes. The greyhound had made the next-door transition just fine, if his snoring was any indicator.

It was mid-evening and I had made the coffee and served up Bettie and Kinder their cups while I also served up the events of the day before, and the story that Bucky Mohler had told me. I didn't dole it out—Bettie seemed able to take it all in as fast as it came. She sat with her hands cradling the coffee cup and the hazel eyes stared into nothing and everything.

"After I talked to Bucky," I said, seated next to Bettie and across from Kinder, "I spent three long hours with the feds."

"Which flavor?" Kinder asked.

"All 57 varieties—the top guy was Homeland Security, but FBI was part of it, another was NSA, and a character who just had to be CIA."

Kinder shrugged. "This does have its foreign implications. What was their take on all this?"

"Their 'take,' " I said with half a smile, "was that I had done more than enough, and they would take it from here."

The captain/manager frowned. "Take what from where?"

"Every aspect of the affair relating to the 'missing materiel'—that's they what called it. They didn't confirm or deny the nuclear aspect."

"Where does that leave us?"

But what Kinder meant was: where does that leave Bettie?

"It leaves us," I said, "with a big old shoe to drop. A big *very* old shoe."

Bettie had said nothing through my report. She hadn't nodded or done anything to indicate these new facts jogged her memory further. Somehow I felt they had—somehow I felt that behind her pretty placid face the wheels were turning. Maybe even spinning.

"You mean the organized crime aspects," Kinder said. "Garrison Properties and Romero Suede and ice cream trucks. You know, one of those trucks, specially rigged, looking innocent as hell, could have hauled that atomic cube down here."

"If they did," I said, "the feds consider that their business." I sipped my own coffee and shrugged. "I gave them everything, Darris—Garrison and Suede and ice cream on a stick. They're probably mounting an operation right now."

"If so, I haven't heard about it."

"We're just the small fry who handed them everything on a platter. But the contents of that old safe don't concern me anymore."

"What does?"

"That shoe. That old shoe."

"That hasn't dropped yet."

"Right."

Kinder's eyes were slits. "And what shoe would that be, Jack?"

And Bettie spoke.

"The floppy discs," she said.

We looked at her. She looked at me. Only the unblinking emptiness of the lovely eyes indicated she wasn't seeing me. *And yet she always saw me....*

"I made copies of those discs for you, Jack," she said calmly.

I sat forward. "Bennie Orbach's insurance policy, you mean? Chapter and verse on the five New York crime families circa twenty years ago...."

She looked away from me, into the past. "Yes. I wasn't just working for Credentials. I had a responsibility to the government, the federal government."

The words were coming steadily but slowly. I tried to help: "You were an expert on computer viruses. You were one of a number of experts, peppered around the country at small computer outfits, helping out the government."

Her eyes opened wider. "Yes. Trying to help avoid and contain near-catastrophic situations."

The officialese mirrored the words of her boss at Credentials.

A funny little smile twisted her lush lips. "I remember, Jack, you used to say, 'Cops hate coincidences.' But it *was* a coincidence, Jack, a complete coincidence that that man Orbach chose Credentials to safeguard his data."

"Do you remember what that data was, Bettie?"

"Just as you said—chapter and verse on the five New York crime families, with an emphasis on the branch he worked for. He pretended to be a writer, a journalist, this man…this Orbach. He claimed much of the material was speculative. And yet he left instructions for the files to go to specific parties in the event of his death by violence or otherwise suspicious circumstances."

I moved my chair closer to hers and slipped an arm around her shoulder. "Do you remember, Bettie? Do you remember where the floppy discs are?"

"I do. Back in New York."

They would be.

She was saying, "We'll have to go there for them. I want to go, too, Jack. I don't want you leaving me behind again—I don't think I could stand it."

"You'll go. *We'll* go."

"As long…as long as we come back here. Because Sunset Lodge is our home."

Kinder had been taking it all in. "Should we call ahead? To your pal Sgt. Ross, maybe? The phones are clean—I saw to it this place was swept for bugs just today."

"No," I said. "This doesn't go anywhere past this table, okay, Darris? Nobody but Bettie, me and you need to know those discs still exist."

I locked eyes with Darris, my expression telling him what my words couldn't risk in front of Bettie: that if the bad guys knew those floppies were around, they'd be on us like fire ants at a picnic.

As I showed Kinder out, I told him to maintain

the surveillance of the house, and he assured me he would.

The lights were mostly out—Bettie didn't need them and I liked the atmosphere. Anyway, we'd left some lights on next door, in Bettie's place, to continue the illusion that she still lived there. So when Bettie led me across into the living room, I bumped into an end table. The blind girl was already more used to my place than I was.

We wound up on the sofa and I sat with my arm around her as she curled up beside and against me. In a sport shirt and slacks, I had to shift a bit to get comfortable because the .45 was still in its holster on my hip, and would stay there for the foreseeable future. Bettie was in white jeans and a pink short-sleeve sweater, the day a little chilly, at least for Florida. The wind off the water was rattling the windows and you could almost remember it was fall in faraway places that weren't drenched in year-round sunshine.

"Where in New York?" I asked her absently. "The discs, I mean. Back at Dr. Brice's place?"

She shook her head. "No. I left them with you."

I stiffened. "You what?"

"The floppies were in my antique desk, the one my grandmother left me. In our apartment, Jack."

She'd had no close living relatives, and as a kid of twenty-one hadn't left a will; the handful of personal items had gone to me, by default.

I turned her toward me. Looked right at her and she gazed at me with the empty hazel eyes. "Bettie… that desk is *here.* It's upstairs, in the bedroom…."

Now she straightened. "Is...is *that* the desk in your bedroom?"

The way she near-echoed me might have been funny in other circumstances. Of course Bettie had got to know the lay of the land or anyway of the furniture in my place. But blind and slowly coming out of memory loss, she had no reason to recognize by touch a desk she hadn't seen in twenty years, even if it was an 18th-century family heirloom.

Still, she was first off the sofa. She went unerringly across the room to the open staircase against the far wall that led up to the master bedroom. I followed. Something about the movement woke Tacos, whose big head craned up to comment by way of a *yip*.

"Stay," I told him, and he settled back down on his braided rug.

In seconds we were up the stairs, onto the landing and into the bedroom.

I threw the overhead light switch, which also started the gentle whirl of the ceiling fan. Like the entire house, the place was under-furnished—just Bettie's old four-poster bed, a nightstand, a chest of drawers and the vintage desk, all among the small load the movers had brought down from the big city.

I moved my swivel chair out of her way, and cleared the bottles off the ornate desk that I'd used for years as a liquor cabinet. Then her fingers began their work.

And those fingers had a memory of their own, finding at once a decorative panel whose fancy carvings disguised a hidden drawer. She had to tug on the chunk of wooden filigree that was a hidden handle a couple of times before it gratingly gave, and screeched open.

Inside was an age-discolored manila envelope, folded over.

She took it out and handed it to me. Within were two floppy discs, the larger size that you don't see often anymore. My name was on the labels. And a word: IMPORTANT.

"All those years," I said, my voice a bitter whisper.

"What, Jack?"

I hefted the lightweight envelope and said, "All those years, I *had* these things—right in my apartment."

She was shaking her head, her lovely dark hair bouncing off her shoulders. "How could you have known? I didn't exactly have time to send a message to you, and later when I *could* have…I couldn't. Because I couldn't remember my own identity, let alone the man I loved."

I hugged her to me. "We need to get out of here right now, doll. We'll grab Kinder and get to the nearest FBI office, and—"

That was when Tacos got back in the act.

Only it wasn't a simple yip, but a yapping, echoing up from downstairs. *The old racing hound was sounding an alarm.*

The .45 was already in my right hand when I got to the window by the bed and looked out and took in an unusual sight for after dark—an ice cream truck double-parked out front. And I hadn't ordered anything sweet.

Simultaneously we said to each other, "We have

company," and there was no time to be impressed by how mutually on the same wavelength we were.

And Tacos was keeping at it, the barking vicious now, ringing off the walls and ceiling downstairs.

I swept Bettie along with me to the bedroom's rear window and looked out across the back yard and between the two houses on our neighboring street, and got a view of another double-parked ice cream truck.

That was when the greyhound's yapping broke off abruptly. The sudden silence sounded its own alarm, one even more troubling than the barking itself.

"Stay here," I whispered.

She didn't argue.

The master bedroom and a sewing room, on the other side of the stairwell, were the only rooms up here on this half a floor. From the landing, I could see nothing of the world below. I paused just long enough to listen for movement, didn't hear any, then started down the stairs cautiously.

The stairs hugged the wall on one side, and were open onto the big living room on the other. Only two lights were on downstairs, a lamp by the sofa and a ceiling fixture over the kitchen table.

As I descended, I could see the fallen Tacos, sprawled on his braided rug, the side of his head matted with blood. He'd been struck a hard blow and he was unconscious but his bony ribcage was rising and falling. Otherwise the living room and the kitchen beyond it appeared empty.

My den was on the other side of the wall the stairs

hugged, under the master bedroom. Beneath the staircase was a bathroom, and a hallway between it and the kitchen led to two guest bedrooms and the laundry room. If intruders were looking for us, they might assume the master bedroom would be downstairs. If they had, I could come up behind them and end this quickly.

That was seeming like a reasonable assumption when a guy in a black stocking-mask and matching wardrobe popped up from where he'd been crouching behind the end table on the far side of the sofa, his form slightly blurred by the light of the lamp, and a silenced shot from a Glock snicked past my ear.

My shot was no snick but an explosion in the open room and then the intruder's head exploded, too, but silently, except for the splat of bone and brain matter that traveled to a window to land and drip.

I spent maybe half a second wondering if the guy was alone but knowing that two ice cream trucks meant multiple salesmen of death, and another one leaned out from behind where the stove and countertop in the kitchen provided him a good position to crouch and shoot.

But before he could, I blasted twice, and one bullet caught his weapon—another silenced Glock—and the other took off some fingers and their little stumps were geysering and he was screaming and when pain and reflex brought him to his feet, my head shot put him out of his misery and brightened up the kitchen cabinets behind him with splashes of red.

When the third black stocking-masked house guest

leapt from the doorway of my den, I ducked and two slugs from another noise-suppressed Glock dug holes in the wood, and I lost my balance and came bump-bump-bumping on my rump down the stairs, firing as did, taking out railing posts but not the intruder, who ducked back in my den, while I hit hard on the little landing, where the stairs took their small four-step jog into the living room.

I'd barely hit up against the railings, including several my .45 had already splintered, when he popped back out and was below me a little and yet right on me, pointing that Glock up at me, but I kicked through the remaining railings and caught him on the chin and sent him back hard against the wall, his Glock popping out of his hand and flying somewhere.

He was helpless against the wall, trying to catch his breath, which was the perfect time to shoot the son of a bitch, but the .45 jammed and then he had his damn breath and reached out and dragged me through the gaping teeth of the landing rails and onto the floor. I landed hard, onto splintered wood, on my back, and he dropped down onto me, landing with his knee in my stomach and all of the air went out of me.

He spoke, but not to me: "Find her. Find the discs."

Somebody said, "Right," and I saw a fourth black-masked figure—where the hell had *he* come from?—go blurring past and on up the stairs. I tried to call out a warning to Bettie, but with my air gone, I had nothing....

The intruder moved the knee to my chest, pinning me there as I gasped for breath, trying to get the hell back in this game. We were in the narrow space at the entry of my den, between the stairway landing and the wall, near the front door.

"Bettie," I said.

But it was barely a whisper.

The man on top of me yanked off his stocking mask. Maybe he was hot. Maybe he wanted to gloat.

For sure he was Romero Suede, a dark pockmarked grinning kid I'd busted more than once and who seemed more at home in this role than selling ice cream to kids and codgers.

"Not such hot shit now," he laughed, "are you, Shooter?"

That was when the lights went out.

Every light in the house, and it startled the man with his knee on my chest, and gave me an edge. I knew this house in the dark, and Suede didn't.

And while my chest was pinned, my arms weren't, and my breath had returned, and I jabbed a short right into his groin, which got his attention. He reared back, letting up on me without meaning to, and I tossed him the hell off of me, and scooted out from under him, then headed up the stairs, toward Bettie and her intruder.

But I took something with me: a chunk of wooden railing with a jagged end. I held the thing in my fist, an eight-inch spear, and when Suede managed to get his bearings enough to come up the stairs after me, and grab onto the back of my shirt, I swung around and jabbed the spear hard, into his heart, like he was a vampire and I was Van Helsing.

He didn't turn into a skeleton and smoke, but he did go away, falling backward and making lots of noise doing it, but not screaming, too dead for that.

And there was noise coming from the master bedroom, terrible noise, including breaking glass. I remembered those bottles and ghastly scenarios were playing out in my mind. I had no weapon now, not even a chunk of stair rail, and the last intruder no doubt had his own damn Glock, but somehow I had to stop him, if only to put myself between him and Bettie, and then I was in the room, ready for anything, except for one thing…

Bettie saying, "*Jack!* I'm fine. Let me get the light."

My mouth was open but nothing was coming out. I could see only darkness in the bedroom and my world was a confused blot until the overhead light went on. Then Bettie was to my right, reaching with one hand into the closet where the fuse box was.

And on the floor was another man in black, masked face down but with a broken bottle of Canadian Club stuck in his back like a handle should anyone want to pick him up. He was shuddering a little, but that didn't last long.

"I figured it was you who turned off the lights," I told her. "But how the hell did you get to those bottles? I put them on the floor, and—"

"And I heard you do it. Heard where you put them. Jack, I feel…numb. I should feel excited or terrible or...glad to be alive, or ashamed to have...killed that man—I *did* kill him, didn't I?"

I was leaning over him now, checking. "Thoroughly. And you may feel bad about it, when you're through being in shock, but you shouldn't. There are three others downstairs just as dead. They were here for you, and me, and those floppy discs."

I went over and slipped my arm around her. "Listen, baby, we're going to hole up here—more may be on the way. In the meantime, I'll get Kinder on the phone, and—"

She squeezed my arm. Whispered, "Jack—someone's in the hall."

Damn! I should have commandeered the dead intruder's Glock, or gone over to the concealed gun closet. And I would have got around to that, but we had company again before I could.

Only the man in the doorway was one of the good guys—Joe Pender. He was in a tan uniform like the one Kinder and the guard at the front gate wore. No cap, though—his red hair, white at the temples, was standing up, like the wind had turned it from hair into flames.

"My God, are you two all right?" He had a Glock in hand too, sans silencer, nose down.

I nodded.

"I've already called Kinder....How many?"

"Four intruders. All dead, or probably so. I haven't checked the other three bodies but you don't recover from what they suffered. Those ice cream trucks still out there?"

"Yes—one here on Kenneth, another back over on

Lawrence. Checked them both before I came in, and they're empty. The drivers must have been part of the house invasion crew."

That was when I saw what I'd been waiting for: *Pender's eyes glancing over at the manila folder on the antique desk.*

"Listen, why don't you get Bettie over next door," Pender said, "and I'll hold the fort down here, till Kinder and backup show. This is a crime scene now."

Bettie sensed something. She had her arm around my waist, and was plastering herself to my side. Her breath was coming slow and hard.

I said, "Joe, mind if I ask you something, before Bettie and I go next door?"

"Sure. But we should—"

"Hurry? Why? Are these stiffs going someplace beside a morgue?"

"No. But I just thought—"

"Here's my question, Joe. You wouldn't happen to be the guy who helped Darris out, and swept this place for bugs, would you? Like you're the guy who suggested I move Bettie next door, so any intruders would be confused about where to go?"

Pender pretended not to see what I was getting at. Didn't do much of a job of it, saying, "Yeah, I swept this place, and as of this morning, it was clean. Land lines, too."

"Here's the thing, Joe. Until those floppies were found, Bettie wasn't a real threat. She's someone who's been watched for years. It hasn't even really been a secret where she's been hiding out. You're even one of the ones who've watched her."

"You're talking crazy, Jack."

I shook my head. "No. What I haven't figured out is how deep you're in it. How far back you go. You don't pull off a major heist like that atomic caper without some inside help in law enforcement, and you were active back then. Hell, we knew each other—you may be the one who told the bastards who snatched Bettie that I'd be at the station house that evening."

"Jack...you're wrong, Jack."

"You were also already starting your side business, of renovating buildings, right? So you may have been the guy who tipped the mob boys off that the urban legend about Big Zappo's big old safe was for real—and that Bucky Mohler owned the building, or at least co-owned it."

His lips were peeled back over his teeth. "I don't even follow this. What kind of medication are you on, Jack?"

"Nothing. I'm in fine shape. The only health scare I've had lately is a Glock in the hand of a bent cop—a cop whose electronic surveillance only this evening, not long ago at all, overheard the discovery of those missing floppy discs. *You* heard it, Joe—heard that last big shoe drop."

And now he stopped denying it. He didn't admit anything, but his expression changed. Hardened. Still, the eyes had a sadness. I'll give him that much—some humanity was still in there.

And, of course, the Glock swung up and aimed itself at me. And Bettie. We were standing so close, we were one damn target.

"One other question, Joe, the eternal one—*why?* You have a nice life down here, and it doesn't even cost you that much. This village is a sweetheart deal for ex-cops. You got a wife who loves you, you got kids, and grandkids, too, right? Why risk it all, why shame yourself and your career, for what? Money?"

Pender sighed. Then he shrugged. "Not that easy, Jack. I've done business with those guys for a long, long time. And I had tastes and habits, when I was younger, that needed underwriting. Gambling. Coke. Pretty young things like your Bettie—*that* you can understand, surely?"

"I understand, Joe. I understand greed and drugs and sex—hell, those are three biggies in our game, right? The big motives? But let me ask you this—how are you going to explain this to Darris, and he'll be here soon—how are you going to explain killing Bettie and me?"

He shrugged and smiled. A sad little smile, but a smile.

"Because I didn't do it. One of those assholes downstairs did—see, this is one of *their* Glocks."

And he extended his arm, pointing the weapon right at me. And Bettie.

He never saw it coming, never sensed the animal leap, the swift, sleek, graceful beast, who saved his snarling for after sinking those sharp teeth tearing into white flesh.

"Back, Tacos!" I said, and the dog, with blood on its face and head—some his own, some Pender's—looked at me with chagrin. Had he been a bad doggie?

"Good boy," I said. "Bettie, take him downstairs. And call Kinder right now—I don't think Joe really did, though with the noise, Darris probably is already on his way."

I went over to where Pender lay in a sprawl, his legs and arms going in directions that had no point, and his eyes were huge and his mouth was bubbling blood and so was his neck, from the jagged open gash, the red streaming.

"Shoo...shoo..." he was saying.

He might have been calling me "Shooter," but I didn't think so.

A trembling finger pointed to the Glock he'd dropped.

When he spoke, it took effort, and you had to give it to him for that, anyway. Of course it was more gurgling than anything else, but I understood.

"Shoo...shoot me," he said.

"Why? You'll be dead in a couple of minutes, Joe. Bleeding out from a wound like that, shouldn't take... oh. I get it. You want me to shoot you with the Glock, and blame it on one of these bastards?"

He managed to nod, the eyes even wider, wilder. With that gash in his neck, you'd think his damn head would've rolled off.

"That way," I said, "your family won't have to suffer. You won't die in disgrace. You went out a good guy, a hero who tried to save Bettie and me."

One more nod and something like hope flickered in the wide eyes.

I stood. "I see where you're coming from, Joe. Trouble is, what about all the *real* good guys, the cops who gave their lives to the Job, and who didn't have mob pals and mistresses and gambling habits and a coke jones? Would be kind of a slap in the face of guys like that. Of guys like me, frankly. It's not that I don't want to shoot you, Joe, but..."

Hell.

He wasn't listening anymore.

So Bettie and I shared the big rocker on my front porch and we watched—or I watched, and she heard—as Captain Darris Kinder and various other real good guys did their cop thing. And a quiet street in a retirement village was suddenly littered with death, as body bags emerged from the house, black cocoons no butterflies would ever exit.

Kinder had finally been contacted by the federal boys. They informed him that a major operation was going down at Garrison Properties. Warrants had been issued, based on info provided by NYPD sources (including a certain retired captain) and a dozen arrests would be made in the early morning hours. Later, we learned these included several high-ranking "retired" Mafiosi, and I was told, off the record, that the long missing "materiel" had at long last been recovered, too.

I pressed, and was told the atomic cube was intercepted when it was being off-loaded from a lead-lined ice cream truck onto a small cruiser at the Garrison Properties dock.

But that was later. Right now Darris Kinder was dealing with a crime scene and all I had to do was cuddle with a beautiful brunette in my lap on a rocker on the front porch.

She fell asleep for a while, after all that excitement. We weren't going to bed, because we had to run Tacos over to the vet as soon as they opened, though right now the greyhound was sleeping peacefully at our feet, tail thumping in a dream as he chased a rabbit, metal or otherwise.

The vehicles had just rolled away when she woke up, snuggled against me even closer, and asked, "Jack—is that the sun coming up?"

"Yes. You want me to describe it?"

"No. I can see it. Not well, but I can see it—colors, shapes. I'm alive, Jack. I'm coming alive."

Soon, so was the street, a boy on a bike hitting porches with papers, retirees in robes collecting them, lights coming on in houses, the sound of radio and TV and even the laughter of children, or anyway grand-children.

The Street back in the big city might be dead, but this one wasn't. All those years without Bettie, I'd been as dead as that ancient patch of pavement. They say retirees go to Florida to die.

But I felt like I was finally starting to live.

THE
END

Following Mickey Spillane Down DEAD STREET

Preparing this novel for publication was a bittersweet task, a thrill, an honor, an obligation, a privilege. My only regret is that the task needing doing.

Back around 1961, I was a thirteen-year-old in Iowa who fell in love with Mickey Spillane's fiction, and was inspired by his work (and that of such peers of his as Dashiell Hammett, Raymond Chandler and James M. Cain) to pursue crime and mystery writing.

As a teenager, I was surprised to learn that the writer I admired so much had been controversial, that in fact he'd been vilified and attacked. When I read about Hammett, Chandler and Cain, I encountered glowing praise for the most part; when I read about Spillane, I heard ridiculous nonsense about pornographic sado-masochism, fascist tendencies and the fostering of juvenile delinquency.

Over the years I became a champion of Mickey's, and I remain so. During the '50s, '60s and into the mid-'70s, Spillane was the world's bestselling author (not mystery writer—*author*, a term he disliked, incidentally) and having to defend a writer so popular seemed absurd to me then, and still does now. Part of my pro-Spillane effort included writing (with James L. Traylor) the first critical study of Spillane's work, *One Lonely Knight: Mickey Spillane's Mike Hammer* (1984), an Edgar Award nominee, and later making a documentary, *Mike Hammer's Mickey Spillane* (1999), available on DVD in the anthology of my short films, *Shades of Noir* (part of the boxed set, *Black Box*).

As a reasonably successful mystery writer identified with championing Spillane, I was asked in 1981 by the organizers of the mystery fan convention, Bouchercon, to serve as their liaison with Mickey, who was one of their honored guests. I was also asked to appear with Mickey on a two-man panel and do the first in-depth public interview of Spillane specifically for mystery fans. Mickey finally coming in close contact with appreciative genre buffs was gratifying to all concerned.

That was when our friendship began, and it lasted until his death in July 2006, and beyond. During those years we worked together on a number of projects, including our comic book series *Mike Danger* and a number of anthologies, some focusing on Mickey's uncollected short fiction, others gathering stories by others in the *noir* tradition Mickey represented. And Mickey did me the favor of appearing as an actor in two of my independent feature films, *Mommy* and *Mommy's Day* (these are also available on DVD).

Additionally, I was privileged to share numerous

conversations with Mickey, both at his home in Murrell's Inlet, South Carolina, and over the phone, about writing. With the exception of Dave Garrity and comic book crony Joe Gill, Mickey had few writer friends. His public persona of the blue-collar writer, self-deprecatingly comparing his work to chewing gum for the masses, meant Mickey allowed few other writers inside the world of craft and art where he spent so much of his life.

No one ever lived who loved storytelling more than Mickey Spillane; no one loved words and vivid turns of phrase more passionately.

Over the last ten or so years of his life, before cancer took him quickly (until his last two months, he was uncommonly healthy for a man in his late eighties), Mickey approached his work in a fashion quite apart from the process of his younger days.

The Spillane of *Kiss Me, Deadly* (1952) wrote quickly, in a fever heat. He claimed to have written some of his novels in intense, brutal sessions of as short a span as three days. *I, the Jury* (1947) may have been done in nine days (although sometimes Mickey admitted to nineteen). This was his habit throughout the '50s and well into the 1970s. He typed with two fingers on cheap yellow paper, single-spaced to "make it look more like a book."

Ideas flowed through Mickey's mind in a manner consistent with his boundless energy, and—during the periods when he didn't publish much (from 1952 to 1961, for example)—he would often noodle with first chapters and story ideas. Sometimes he would come back to these, other times not. In his last ten years, his habit was to work in three offices in his home (one was actually outside his house, a small shack on stilts). Often he would have a book going in each.

The last Spillane novel published during his lifetime, the adventure yarn *Something's Down There* (2003), was one of these—he had begun it in the late seventies or early eighties, and didn't finish it till a month or so before he submitted it. During his last five years he had four novels going—two Mike Hammers (*The Goliath Bone* and *King of the Weeds*), an adventure novel (*The Last Stand*) and a crime novel (*Dead Street*).

Mickey completed *The Last Stand*, and had done extensive work on the other three, moving back and forth between them as his muse dictated. A major frustration of his last two months was that he wanted to finish *Goliath Bone* in particular, as he had promised himself and fans "the last Mike Hammer" in which Hammer and his loyal secretary, Velda, would finally marry.

These last four novels show Mickey—who definitely had a sense of both his mortality as a man and his immortality as a writer—returning to the three genres he loved: private eye, adventure, and crime. For the latter, he in particular liked to write about tough cops, as witness *The Deep* (1961), *Killer Mine* (1968) and *The Last Cop Out* (1973).

Initially, Hard Case Crime editor Charles Ardai and I were going to publish *The Last Stand* first, as it was the final work Mickey completed. The book is a very entertaining rumination on friendship and is thematically about as typically Spillane as anything he ever wrote; but the adventure-tale nature of the story itself is more on a par with *Something's Down There* than the mystery/crime novels with which Mickey was so strongly identified.

So while *The Last Stand* will no doubt see print before long, Charles and I—with Jane Spillane's blessing—decided to start here, with Mickey's final cop/crime novel. As this novel is a rare look at the later years of a traditional hardboiled anti-hero, and opens with (and periodically returns to) poetic musings on life, death and re-birth in and out of the big city, *Dead Street* seems the perfect novel to remind readers why Mickey Spillane was the 20th century's bestselling, most famous writer of "tough guy" fiction.

Mickey and I spoke many times about *Dead Street*. On several of my visits to his home over the last ten years, this was the book he was working on. It began as a much different animal, although with common elements—originally, he intended to write about four ex-cops and their wives in a Florida retirement community oriented to police and firemen (based on a real such village), and crimes they solved in the area. As *Dead Street* evolved into his more typical loner cop story, Mickey often said he thought it would make a good movie for older actors, and hoped Charles Bronson might play the lead and that Lee Meredith, Mickey's co-star in the incredibly long-running Miller Lite commericials, might play the blind girl, Bettie.

Friendship was key in Mickey's work and, of course, his life. Jack Stang, the hero of this novel, takes the name of the real-life upstate New York cop who was one of Mickey's best friends, and who Mickey had hoped would one day play Mike Hammer in the movies. Mickey even shot a short try-out film for Stang as Hammer in the '50s, and Stang appears with Mickey in the John Wayne produced film, *Ring of Fear* (1954), available on DVD. The irony is that Mickey blew Stang off the screen in that film, and set the stage for playing Hammer himself in *The Girl Hunters* (1963).

Toward the end of his life, Mickey realized he would not be able to finish these last few novels, and he indicated to me that after he was gone, these and other unfinished projects would be turned over for me to complete. I later learned that he'd said to his wife Jane, "Give all this stuff to Max—he will know what to do with it."

No greater honor could have been paid to me by my friend, with the possible exception of the day he consented to be my son Nathan's godfather.

Most of *Dead Street* is Mickey's—eight of eleven chapters are his work, with minor additions and continuity corrections by me based upon his notes. Mickey famously said he didn't rewrite, but this was not entirely accurate: he did modest line edits and rather major inserts, adding material where later plot developments required earlier clarification.

Often Mickey wrote the ending first, or at least a rough version of it; but that was not the case with *Dead Street*. He did, however, leave extensive notes ranging from plot concerns to characterization, and I was able to figure out where he was heading and what he was intending. The last few chapters I fashioned from those notes, and from conversations about *Dead Street* that Mickey and I had over the last several years.

I wish to thank Mickey's wife Jane for her support and confidence, and for her willingness to dig and search for every scrap of *Dead Street* notes available (and these were extensive). I'd also like to thank my producing partner, Ken Levin; Mickey's typist, Vickie Fredericks; Jane's attorney David Gundling; and agent Dominick Abel. And, of course, thank you to Barbara Collins, my wife and frequent collaborator, who helped Jane and me conduct the "treasure hunt" among Mickey's papers.

Charles Ardai of Hard Case Crime had been in touch with Mickey during the last year or so of the writer's life, and Mickey was greatly impressed with what the Hard Case line was accomplishing. I know he would be pleased to have *Dead Street* published here in the company of such writers he admired as Ed McBain, Lawrence Block and Donald E. Westlake.

Finally, of course, I must thank Mickey for his friendship, his influence and his faith in me. And for ensuring that a certain part of me remains at all times Mickey Spillane's biggest thirteen-year-old fan.

Max Allan Collins
October 2006
Muscatine, Iowa

About the Author

MICKEY SPILLANE, creator of private eye Mike Hammer, was the bestselling American mystery writer of the 20th century, and likely the most influential. He was also the most widely translated fiction author of the 20th century, although he insisted he was not an "author," but a writer.

A bartender's son, Mickey Spillane was born in Brooklyn, New York, on March 9, 1918. An only child who swam and played football as a youth, Spillane got a taste for storytelling by scaring other kids around the campfire. After a truncated college career, Spillane—already selling stories to pulps and slicks under pseudonyms—became a writer in the burgeoning comic-book field (*Captain America*, *Submariner*), a career cut short by World War II. Spillane—who had learned to fly at air strips as a boy—became an instructor of fighter pilots.

After the war, Spillane converted an unsold comic book project—*Mike Danger, Private Eye*—into a hard-hitting, sexy novel. The $1,000 advance was just what the writer needed to buy materials for a house he wanted to build for himself and his young wife on a patch of land in Newburgh, New York.

The 1948 Signet reprint of his 1947 E.P. Dutton hardcover novel, *I, the Jury*, sold in the millions, as did the six tough mysteries that soon followed; all but one featured hard-as-nails P.I. Mike Hammer. The Hammer thriller *Kiss Me, Deadly* (1952) was the first private eye novel to make the *New York Times* best-seller list.

Much of Mike Hammer's readership consisted of Spillane's fellow World War II veterans, and the writer—in a vivid, even surrealistic first-person style—escalated the sex and violence already intrinsic to the genre, in an effort to give his battle-scarred audience hard-hitting, no-nonsense entertainment. For this blue-collar approach, Spillane was attacked by critics and adored by readers. His influence on the mass-market paperback was immediate and long lasting, his success imitated by countless authors and publishers. Gold Medal Books, pioneering publisher of paperback originals, was specifically designed to tap into the Spillane market.

Spillane's career was sporadic; his conversion in 1952 to the conservative religious sect, the Jehovah's Witnesses, is often cited as the reason he backed away, for a time, from writing the violent, sexy Hammer novels. Another factor may be the enormous criticism heaped upon Hammer and his creator. Spillane claimed only to write when he needed the money, and in periods of little or no publishing, Spillane occupied himself with other pursuits—flying, traveling with the circus, appearing in motion pictures, and for nearly twenty years spoofing himself and Hammer in a lucrative series of Miller Lite beer commercials.

The controversial Hammer has been the subject of a radio show, a comic strip, and two television series, starring Darren McGavin (in the late '50s) and Stacy Keach (in the mid-'80s with a 1997 revival, both produced by Spillane's friend and partner, Jay Bernstein). Numerous gritty movies have been made from Spillane novels, notably director Robert Aldrich's seminal film *noir*, *Kiss Me Deadly* (1955), and *The Girl Hunters* (1963), starring Spillane himself as his famous hero.

The sometime actor also appeared in two independent films (*Mommy*, 1995, and *Mommy's Day*, 1997) written and directed by his mystery writer friend, Max Allan Collins.

Mickey Spillane died in July 2006, joining the ranks of Dashiell Hammett, Raymond Chandler and Agatha Christie, arguably the only other mystery writers of the 20th century with comparable name recognition.